To
all th ^
from one writer to another
Doz Barden

The Gift

by
D.E Barden

Printed in the United Kingdom

First Printing: July 2018
Biddles: www.biddles.co.uk/

ISBN 978 1 912804 15 3

Foreword

I wrote this book in memory of the countless young teenagers
I taught in my time as their English teacher at Sackville School,
East Grinstead. They showed me that a book should have mystery,
terror, danger and excitement mixed with humour and fun. Here,
Jonno and Bomber embark on a hazardous journey which tests their
courage and quick wits to the limit.

My thanks go to Tracy, who typed everything for me and without
whom I could not have managed, to many of my students
whose exploits I have used and to my family, especially my seven
grandchildren all of whom are thinly disguised in the story.
Dot Barden

Contents

Chapter 1. What Lies Beneath

"Bomber?"

"What?"

"I'm hungry"

"So, what's new?"

"No, really hungry, dead starving, famished."

"Come off it, you had eggs, bacon and –"

"No, not that food – what we used to have, you know, a Big Mac, a pizza from that shop on the corner, dripping with cheese and –"

"Shut up, Jonno, before I deck you."

"Well, I'm fed up (ha ha) with chicken casserole, roast and all that gunge, I want real food, fish and chips, kebabs, fries…"

"Jonathon, you don't seem to be eating your dinner. Is there something wrong?"

"No, Uncle Jim, it's just that I'm not very hungry",

"You won't want any strawberry ice cream then?"

"I guess not."

"Not 'guess', Jonathon, you mean 'suppose'.

"I suppose so, Uncle Jim".

"Uncle Jim"

"Yes, David, what do you want?"

"Can Jonathan and I go to the library? I don't want any afters either."

"Of course, I'm always delighted to see the library being used."

"I can't get used to you being called David."

"Neither can I. I can't remember anyone except my first teacher calling me that. Right from the word go I was 'Bomber because of my surname being Lancaster'.

"What a relief to be away from that place"

"I don't think the Uncles would like to hear you call it that – not that I disagree with you, what with the smell of fish pie – it's disgusting"

"Anyway, what's on your mind? Why did you want the library? You don't like the selection of books here anymore than I do".

"Listen, this is important and I didn't want anyone listening. I want you and me to get away from here"

"You mean, run off, escape?"

"Got it in one."

"When?"

"Soon as we can. I've already worked out a plan. We leave on a Saturday night. The Uncles are always late to bed that night and sometimes Uncle Jim doesn't even come to bed and even if he does, he goes straight to his cubicle and doesn't check up on us."

"How do we get out? Even if the cameras don't pick us up crossing the playground or the fields, how do we get over the perimeter fence? It's about 20 feet high. And, even if we manage it, where would we go?"

"How the hell do I know! Anywhere that's not here. Don't you want to get away from this prison?"

"It's not that bad. We get fed even if the grub is boring, it's an easy life – a bit dull I know, but it beats being out there, sleeping rough, no food, weirdos everywhere."

"Come off it – think how the other half live, take aways, on the settee watching good stuff on T.V and all that. Do you want to come or not? It'd be fun, an adventure. You must see that."

"Well, I do remember some good things from way back and I suddenly realised the other night how weird this place is."

"How do you mean?"

"Well after supper on Monday, Uncle Bill told me to fetch a box of baked bean cans from the pantry."

"So?"

"When I found the beans, I was about to leave when I heard a car directly outside."

"What's weird about a car?"

"Don't be thick. Did you hear me – a car outside on the same level as the food store – no windows on that floor or on the next one up. All the rooms we use start on the next floor, 3 up from outside.

2

The hall, the dorms, snooker room."

"So, what about it? The gym is on the ground floor with no windows, only bright lights and air con, which makes sense with all the balls and stuff flying about."

"I still think it's a bit weird, makes the place seem like a prison, if you see what I mean."

"Not really, since we can go outside whenever we want to, dick head."

"Only in the day."

"Come off it – do you really want to be out there after dark?"

Jonno was in the Other Place, in a schoolroom. A voice was talking to him. He couldn't see who it was, but the voice sounded like Uncle Victor, the English teacher back at the Home.

"What can you tell me about Chaucer, Jonathon?"

"He was a famous poet, lived in the 14th century. His most famous stuff was 'The Canterbury Tales'. He pretended that about 30 people were on a pilgrimage to the shrine of St Thomas a Becket in Canterbury Cathedral. Most of the 'pilgrims' were ordinary people who just wanted to have a laugh on the way there, getting drunk, meeting new people and swapping stories to keep everyone entertained on the way from London to Canterbury."

"Good, which tales have you read?"

"Three so far. My favourite is 'The Miller's Tale' it's about..."

"I'm sure you're well acquainted with that one. Which others have you studied?"

"I like the 'Pardoner's Tale'. There's plenty of action. Three idiots get pissed and go on a rampage to kill Death. Everyone in Chaucer's time turns ideas into people so they find an old man and think he is Death. He tells them there is treasure under a tree and the 3 of them are so greedy they don't want to share it so they kill each other and not one finds the treasure."

"A fair summary but don't forget that for your GCSE question you will be expected to show a good understanding of his language and

to put it into context of its time etc."
"I know. I already did a question on the 'Nun's Priest's Tale' in the
mocks and I got an A*, so no worries."
"True. You can go out and relax now."
Jonno walked out into sunshine and went fast across the field to
his favoured place, a deep pool formed by an offshoot of the river
where the water lingered and was warmed by the sun. He stripped
off and straightaway belly flopped in. Soon the mud on the bottom
oozed through his toes like melted chocolate and the fronds of fern
brushed against his face as he floated, eyes closed. A shadow, his
eyes wide open, silhouette, black against the sun. "Who are you?"
Nothing there, vanished, not imagination, he knew it wasn't. But,
whatever it was, or who it was, had gone. Shuddering, he dressed,
eyed the nearby thin copse for any sign of hidden watchers. Again,
nothing. Sun behind clouds, storm in the offing, things fuzzy round
the edges, time to leave..

"Bomber, could you help with my Maths homework?"
"You want me to do it as usual?"
"Not exactly, this time; I just want you to check my working."
"In other words, do it for you."
"No! Well, yes – but might I remind you of my input in your essay on
'Lord of the Flies'"
"OK, you have a point, but don't hang about. It's 20 to 9 already."
After Maths, it was Biology, favourite lesson for all 25 of the boys.
No one ever feigned a head ache or belly ache when Mr Robson,
the visiting Biology tutor was due. He was one of the few 'outside'
teachers who taught a subject for GCSE. Most of the lessons were
taken by the Uncles. Only Mandarin Chinese, Russian and, of
course, Biology were given to visiting specialists. Mr Robson was
a clear winner with the boys. For a start, they loved his clothes. He
was always untidy; jackets of uncertain age with occasional safety
pins instead of buttons, socks that didn't match and hair tied back

in a ponytail. But, above all they enjoyed his lessons. Like all the best teachers, he loved his subject and enthusiastically set about transferring his delight in all things biological to his charges. As he described the workings of the Inner Ear, the boys could see the otoliths, the little chalk balls, racing round the semi-circular canals like bikes round a velodrome. Best of all, each week he brought in something from his prep cupboard in the Biology lab of the state comprehensive school where, as head of Biology, he taught for the rest of the week. Aware that the Uncles might be disapproving, he would whisper in conspiratorial fashion towards the end of the two hour session; "As you've been so good, chaps, would you like to see something from my cupboard?" The boys would sit, shivering slightly with excitement tinged with a light frisson of dread – some of Mr Robson's exhibits were a touch frightening.

Three weeks ago, Jonno, Bomber and the others had waited expectantly for their treat and had stared, puzzled, at the large bell jar he produced with something preserved in formaldehyde and then saw with horror that a huge tapeworm (11ft long) was coiled round a stick, glistening pale and with the mouth and suckers intact. "I extracted it myself from the pig's anus," he gleefully told his awe struck audience; It was all too much for Fungus, one of the boys, who promptly passed out. Luckily, Bomber slapped him smartly on the cheek and he sat up quickly and, after being sternly warned by the rest of the group to keep quiet about the whole thing, he was soon back to normal. Afterwards he excused himself by declaring that he "felt sorry for the tapeworm".
This week, it was time for their treat and Mr Robson did not disappoint. He produced 2 slightly shrivelled pear shaped objects. Fungus was curious, "What are they, Sir?"
"Can anyone guess what they are?"
"Give us a clue, Sir."
"O.K. They belong to something I'm very fond of".

"What are you very fond of, Sir?"

"Well, take your pick from; my motorbike, my camera, my friends, my parents, trees, my dog and—"

Fungus had one of his occasional flashes of inspiration. 'My dog' did it for him.

"I think I know. They are your dog's bollocks, aren't they, Sir?"

"Got it in one, Fungus, well done. They are indeed my dog's testicles or bollocks as you so colourfully put it."

"That seems very cruel, Sir."

"Not at all, Fungus, he's happier without them"

"I wouldn't be happier without mine."

What promised to be an interesting discussion was forestalled by the bell for the end of the lesson and the arrival of Uncle Joe with the announcement that there were iced buns and cocoa for the class and coffee for Mr Robson in the hall.

"That was a good lesson."

"Yeah, not so sure about the next one, though."

"Oh, Chinese is OK."

"It's just that it gives me brain ache, it's so hard."

"Worth it, though. You know as well as I do, that Chinese is where it's all happening; and Germany. That's why we have to do German."

"I know that, geek head. Like Mr Robson said, all the GCSE subjects we do here are going to be very useful in the future."

"I've realised why the Uncles 'rescued' some of us and not everyone."

"What do you mean, Jonno?"

""Think about it. You and I were both in that squat, doing quite well for ourselves. Then Uncle Jim arrived, only we didn't know he was Uncle Jim and I've just realised, or anyway I realised last night when I was thinking about things, that he only took you and me."

"Well, let's face it, we are fantastic!"

"No seriously. You remember how many boys were there with us?"

"Four others, why?"

6

"Think about it. Before we knew who he was, he used to talk to us, remember, about serious things, politics and stuff, films and art, books."

"You're right. Remember that night he asked us all about Pythagoras Theorem – you know the stuff about the square on the hypotenuse being equal to the sum of---".

"Of course, I remember. I'm not an idiot."

"Exactly, that's my point. Only us two could do it, the other 4 didn't know what the hell he was talking about."

"Your point being?"

"You must see what I mean. The Uncles haven't randomly picked us. They have deliberately chosen clever ones."

"Big head!"

"No, I'm not being big headed. It's true. Everyone here can do all the difficult subjects. Everyone can do Chinese and Jed and Darko are doing Russian with Uncle Ross. We get pissed off sometimes with all the hard stuff, but we can do it."

"I suppose you're right. Now I come to think of it, they don't teach us any of the easy subjects for GCSE here – none of what we called the soft options."

"That's right – no Media Studies – all the dumbos chose that because everyone got at least a C."

"Yeah. Last time I was at ordinary school – it seems ages ago, now – I remember some kid in year 10 telling me it was the only subject he had a cat in hell's chance of passing."

"So, to get back to what I was saying."

"Yes, you were wittering on about us all being Einsteins here – Why is it, do you think?"

"That's what I'm wondering, after all, this is supposed to be a home for boys who are homeless or who have run away. On the website it says 'Oakhurst, a residential home for disadvantaged boys aged 11-16' so why is it just for very intelligent boys?"

"I'd not really thought about it but now I come to think about it, the whole set up is weird. We are all taking at least 12 GCSEs and most of us have already taken some."

"Yeah – Jed and Darko passed Russian in year 9 and are taking AS Level this year – mind you, Darko is half Russian."

"Jed isn't though, he's a bit of a mongrel, a bit of French, a bit of German, some Irish and maybe English as well."

"You took Maths in year 8, didn't you?"

"So's nearly everyone."

"Except me; I'm taking it this year. It's always been my weakest link."

"You're OK at it, though, even if you do need my help from time to time."

"D' you reckon we could snitch another iced bun? I need sustenance to see me through Chinese."

"No need to snitch one, it's Big Sue on break duty today and she fancies you."

"What the hell are you talking about?"

"Come off it, you know very well she does. Who always gets the biggest slice of chocolate cake and the most chicken and mushroom pie and the most humungous—"

"Shut it or I'll stuff it in your gob."

"Why are you going red then? OK OK, no need to get violent. Anyway I want another bun too, so I'll ask."

After Chinese, which as Jonno had predicted, had been quite testing, some of the boys spent the time before the evening meal relaxing in the games room. Spike and Tom-Tom, both snooker fanatics, were engaged in serious contest at the table in the middle of the room. Four or five others were lazily watching them. The rest were in the adjoining gym playing a lively game of basketball. Jonno, leaping energetically round the court, still managed to consider again the structure of the home. He now thought it odd like Bomber that there were no proper windows until the second floor. The gym and games room and various store rooms on the ground floor had mere slits near ceiling level, likewise the first floor which was comprised of two or three rooms used as offices and a large utility room with 3 fan extractors. Once, when the boys had been taken for a survival weekend to the nearby hills, they had camped in make shift tents in freezing February and were told to make breakfast. They had been given only matches, the rest was up to them. After begging new laid eggs from a nearby sympathetic farmer's wife, they found a rusty tin can, collected twigs and dried leaves to make a rather reluctant fire, then they scrambled eggs in the tin and made charred and smoky toast with the sliced bread that Flat Freddie had stolen from the pantry the previous day. He was named Flat Freddie after Flat Stanley, a character in a well-loved children's story who was so thin he could be lowered down into drains to rescue dropped money or rings and who, on one occasion, was put in a picture frame in an art gallery in order to catch an art thief. After the burnt but, nevertheless, tasty breakfast, Jonno and a few others climbed the steep slope to the summit of the highest crag and surveyed the landscape. They could see their home nestling in the otherwise empty landscape, empty of building that is, apart from a reservoir building in the far distance. The trees and bushes surrounding the lawn and grassy badminton court were mostly thick fir trees and clipped rhododendron bushes and in Jonno's eyes they seemed to be guarding the house. If he looked too hard they moved imperceptibly closer as if to prevent any one breaking in – or out.

Outside the trees and bushes were the playing fields, a football pitch, long jump and a cricket pitch and pavilion, all encircled by a running circuit which in turn was surrounded by a very high perimeter fence. Without the fence, the whole place would have looked like a pleasant country estate or a rather expensive exclusive boarding school. However, the fence altered its character completely, even though luxuriant pink and blue hydrangea bushes and rampant ivy round the house concealed the windowless walls of the first two floors. The huge iron gates at the entrance, not visible from where Jonno stood, were almost always closed and were entry coded, anyway. As he skivvied with the rest of his fellow sufferers waiting for Uncle Joe to arrive and having checked they had successfully pitched camp and breakfasted, to give the order to return home. Jonno considered his plan to leave in a warmer month with Bomber and possibly Tom-Tom who was good at direction finding, equally as efficient as a sat-nav and without their annoying voices. Tom-Tom could be trusted not to give the game away but he wasn't physically very strong and fit, being prey to asthma attacks and bronchitis.

Come summer Jonno longed to be outside again, to wander round streets, familiar or unfamiliar, full of life and colour, to run and jump and climb on walls, fences and steps, to climb trees in deep countryside, to swim in ponds and rivers, explore derelict houses – all the things he'd done before Uncle 'rescued' him from his wild life with Bomber and the other 4. True, he thought, we were often hungry, sometimes cold and occasionally really scared when we invaded the space of some vicious weirdos. Our gang managed pretty well though. People fell for Bomber's big dark eyes and gave him loads of stuff and one of the others was really brilliant at nicking stuff. We called him the Artful Dodger – never knew his other name. He taught us how to fool the shopkeepers, dodge the cameras and where to get food for free – from the supermarket bins just after closing time.

Evening meal. The dining hall was warm and bright. July sunlight flooded the round tables where the boys sat and the polished table on a raised dais where the Uncles dined. In spite of Jonno's assertion that the hall was pervaded by the odour of cabbage, this evening smelt of roast beef and crispy roast potatoes. The boys happily devoured their roast dinner, after going to the hatch where Big Sue readily handed out 'seconds'. For 'afters' they could choose between chocolate ice cream or sponge pudding with custard. Some even managed both. When he thought about things honestly, Jonno could see the good points about the home, namely the food, the warmth in the winter, the friendship of the other boys and, as for the Uncles, if he was honest, they were helpful and never lost their tempers. And, of course, there was the teaching. I'd miss doing my exams, mused Jonno to himself. On the plus side I've already done GCSE English, German and Geography this June and hope to get an A or A*. Well the Uncles reckon I will anyway, I've already got an A* in history and French. I'll be sorry not to sit Biology, Physics and Chemistry next year, but I've done most of the syllabus and Uncle says I'm already fluent in Mandarin. Should be enough to get me by, perhaps a job translating in a Chinese take-away.

Later. Jonno is in the garden near the house. Bomber and Tom-Tom are with him.
"Bomber, have you thought any more about what I said – about getting out of here, I mean?"
"Ye-es, I have and I'm not sure."
"Why?"
"Well, I like the idea of an adventure, like escaping at dead of night and it would be good to be outside again, like, free."
"What's stopping you, then?"
"I quite like it here, it's much more comfortable than living outside. I like having regular meals and a warm bed. Christ, you know how bloody freezing it is outside some nights."
"It won't be freezing now – in July."
"Don't give me that, Jonno – anyway, it can still rain damn hard in July. Another thing, I still want to take the rest of my GCSEs next year. Like you, I've still got the 3 sciences and Mandarin to do."
"I know, but think about it. With what you've already done, you'll get a job when you're 16. Most kids get about 10 subjects and not many get all As or A*s. What about you, Tom-Tom?"
"No way! I like it here."
"Even if you're a sort of prisoner?"

"I don't care. I hated being outside. I couldn't cope like you probably did. I left home – my mum had a new bloke. He moved in and he hated me, wanted me out of the way, used to beat me up when she was at work. He was out of work so he was always there. I was scared. I met up with 2 boys older than me. They made me take packets of stuff to people they called their customers. I found out it was drugs and I was terrified of being caught so when Uncle Ben asked me if I would like to come here, I did."

"O.K Tom-Tom, but would you do us a favour?"

"Just a minute, Jonno, I haven't said I'm coming," interrupted Bomber.

"But you will, Bomber, I know you will. You can't resist an adventure, can you?"

"True, but I'm still not convinced that we'd even make it out of here. What about the fence if we even made it that far?"

"I've made a recce last time I did 3 laps round the running track. There's a point where a massive bush hides you from the house and if I could get wire cutters from the shed I could cut a hole big enough in no time."

"Are you sure you'd find wire cutters?"

"Maybe not, but there's sure to be something similar. Uncle Frank is always cutting something around the place and the shed is hardly ever locked."

"But, where would we go if we did make it outside?"

"That's where we need you, Tom-Tom."

"Count me out. No way am I coming with you."

"O.K. But I still need your help."

"How?"

"You know why we call you Tom-Tom – because you're so bloody good at map reading, orienteering and all that stuff."

"So?"

"Well, where are we here – somewhere down in the West Country?"

"Yes, I've worked out we're in the countryside about 6 miles from

Penzance."

"How do you know?"

"From things I've heard the Uncles say and names and places I've seen on delivery vans. Anyway, you must remember the places we've been to on our days out and the time it's taken to get there. Last month we went to that working museum with a tin mine mock-up, didn't we, for a science trip? Well the journey was less than an hour and I spotted a signpost to Liskeard, 7 miles."

"So – where's that?"

"In Cornwall, thicko."

"O.K. So you're a human sat-nav and that's where you come in. Even if you're not coming with us, I want you to plan our journey for us, for me and Bomber."

"Where are you aiming for?"

"For a little village called Runcton just outside Chichester in West Sussex."

"Surely you want to go back home to London?"

"Why would I? My family disowned me and, anyway, I hate London. When I was very young we all went on holiday to Runcton and we did bed and breakfast in this really good place. The house had a big orchard outside with lovely old apple trees, long grass with millions of chickens wandering about laying eggs. The man and woman who ran it let me climb the trees and look for nests of eggs in the grass. I had to collect then in a basket. It was great finding the warm brown eggs. I loved it there, it was the best place in the world and Auntie and Uncle (that's what I called them) were the best people in the world. I know they'd take us in, Bomber, if we could get there."

"You're beginning to convince me. When do we go?"

"Things to do first. Like collect a few things to take with us, matches, some food, gear for if it rains and this is where you come in, Tom-Tom."

"You need me to prepare your itinerary, a sort of map with places to recognise?"

"Got it in one! No need to start it till beyond Exeter because when Uncle Jim took us all by train there, I worked out how easy it would be to get on a train at any of the stations before Exeter and escape without going through the barrier."

"What about ticket inspectors?"

"Easy. They don't always come down the train and even if they do we can keep moving and hiding from them."

"Easier said than done, I reckon, but I'm willing to give it a try."

Tom-Tom set about his task straightaway, delighted to be doing one of his favourite things – working with maps, especially ordnance survey maps. He loved decoding the symbols and could visualise the landscape before him in 3D. He could see the quarries, the abandoned tunnels, hidden behind a small copse, the ruined follies the abandoned villages, the war department areas, forbidden territory with a big red DANGER scrawled across it like graffiti. He imagined himself wild swimming in secret pools, once part of large stately homes turned into care homes, their gardens neglected, where he could wander at will. He, therefore, hurried to the Geography room, which was well stocked with ordnance survey maps and took a selection to the quiet room where he was sure he would be undisturbed as it was the time of day when the Uncles would either be out for the evening or relaxing in their own quarters. Taking Jonno at his word he began the itinerary at Exeter, plotting several different maps with, instead of reference symbols, careful and imaginative tiny drawing of various points of interest along the way. His particular favourite was the A272 which he decided would be a good option as it ran from the West Country, well Stockbridge anyway, towards the Chichester area, by way of Petersfield, Midhurst and Petworth and had some great eccentric places and building around it to the North and South.

He worked hard at his task for over a week, making sure that none, neither Uncle or boys, knew what he was doing. If anyone enquired why he was so busy, he explained he was busy on a Geography project. This was accepted without question as, in spite of their varied backgrounds, there was a strong tradition of hard work and an even stronger desire to do very well in exams. He also made sure that all the maps were replaced each day, early in the morning, lest the Uncle should need them for a lesson.

Finally, the folder of various possible routes was completed, with all the places which Tom-Tom, anyway, found interesting, shown as little drawings in coloured inks. He put them all in a wallet folder and gave them to Jonno.

"These look great, Tom-Tom, in fact they are unbelievable. I want to follow all the routes, but these are all brilliant. Why don't you come with us?"

"It's tempting, but not that tempting. I don't want to leave here. I like it and I'm staying. I like my comforts and, anyway, I want to go to Big Home to do 'A' Levels and go on to University. Where else could we have it all paid for us?"

Jonno replied thoughtfully, "Exactly, where else? Which makes me wonder why this whole place is doing all this for us?"

"Because it's a charity, of course, like taking us off the streets and all that."

"I still think there's a hidden agenda at the end of the line. Why do they only want boys who can pass exams easily and who can cope with learning Chinese and Russian?"

"I can't answer that. I only know I'm staying here."

Jonno and Bomber had plenty to do in the way of preparing for the Great Escape. Jonno realised it would not be easy. He reasoned that the best time would be soon after the boys were asleep and Uncle had gone away for the weekend. He had overheard Uncle discussing his plans to visit friends the following Friday for the whole weekend and as it was already the Sunday before, he had to move fast.

He and Bomber were outside again in the garden, apparently lazily watching four of the boys playing badminton on a net placed on the grass. The July evening was warm and still. A cloud shaped like a hedgehog hung in the sky and a crescent moon already showed palely in the blue.

"I've collected matches, Bomber and I had a bit of luck, yesterday. I had to fetch some stuff for Big Sue from the store and guess what was staring me in the face?"

"A rat?"

"Oh, very droll. No – a groundsheet and on one of the shelves, packs of rations for when we go night orienteering. Remember they are quite tasty. We had them when we did that survival weekend ages ago. Anyway, I nicked as many as I could and I've hidden them in an empty locker in the dorm. All we need to do, now, is suss out whether there are any traps when we cross the garden, field and running track."

"If you like, I'll do a dummy run this evening. I'm quicker and quieter than any of you lot so I'll check it out, see if I can spot any booby traps or Rottweilers."

Bomber lay motionless in bed waiting till he thought the others would be asleep. He had expected to feel nervous but instead tremors of excitement ran through him like electric currents. He realised that the comfortable life in the Home had softened him and now – now he was elated, on a mission. Sensing Jonno's tension in the nearby bed, he slid silently out of bed, crossed to the door, purposely left ajar earlier, and was outside in the quietness of the corridor. Making it to the stairs, dimly lit, and to the ground floor was easy. Finding the side door to the outside, not quite so easy. For one thing it was bolted with a very heavy and rusty bar which looked as if it had not been used for years, decades even. Carefully he heaved at the bar trying to move it soundlessly. Sweating, he eventually succeeded, opened the door and stepped outside.

He remained still while he attempted to find his bearings. Everything was still and although the night was cloudy, the nearly full moon gave a luminescence that allowed Bomber to see the outlines of the bushes and trees on the gardens and field in front of him.

"I've got to reach that group of trees to my right," Bomber mused to himself. "I know that massive rhododendron bush is in front of the little shed where they keep the badminton stuff. I'll make for that." He was about to step out when he heard a low, deep rumbling almost like distant thunder but not quite. Whatever it was, it was growing louder. Bomber stood in the doorway, uncertain. After a few moments the sound gradually faded. Bomber stepped noiselessly from the door, closed it and set out, first crossing the immediate lawns till he reached the bushes and small evergreen trees which separated the lawns from the playing fields beyond. The bushes which always seemed like guards were even more oppressive in the faint light of night time. "Shit, I'm sure that bush moved. Get a grip – course it didn't." Nevertheless, as he moved through the encircling trees, his heart thumped and he was frightened. However, he reached the circular running track after crossing the games field at the gallop and looking neither left nor right. The running track gleamed dully but searching for the concealing bush by the perimeter fence was not easy. For a start everything by the fence was shadowy. "I'll have to walk round the track to look for it," he thought. "Not much fun. I'm right out in the open here. Anyone or anything can see me." He suddenly wondered why he had said 'anything'. The excursion, begun as an adventure, became fearful, full of hidden danger. Now he did not want to find the concealing bush; concealing what? Then, with heart jumping out of his chest, clammy with cold sweat down his back, he saw the bush, standing aggressively between the track and the fence. Bomber could not look behind it – Jonno would have to accept that it was fit for purpose.

The journey back was uneventful – and fast. As he pulled the bed clothes over him he was still shivering and sweaty. In the morning as they showered and dressed, Jonno eagerly accosted him.

"Well, did you find it? Was it all OK?"

"Fine – the bush we want is in a direct line if you face the running track by the starting post."

"Good, that means we can go this weekend, on Saturday night. Everything's on our side that night. I've looked it up – it's a full moon tonight. We don't want that, everyone could see us, but on Saturday it rises very late, well after we've gone."

"Yes, and I've just realised, some of the boys are away that weekend, at Stratford-on-Avon. They're leaving by coach on Friday. Uncle Jim and Uncle Dan will be with them, so no one looking after our dorm. Right?"

"Right. I can't wait. This will be such a great gag."

"Where do we go when we get out?"

"We just run as far as we can before day light. We'll find a quiet road and hitch a lift before anyone here realises we've scarpered."

"Spike and China will see we've gone when they wake up."

"Doesn't matter. You don't watch enough detective shit on T.V. If you did you'd know the value of red herrings."

"I know about red herrings, I'm not dumb."

"Well I've planted a few. I've told Spike and co that you and me are going on an early morning fishing trip down by the weir and we won't be back till lunchtime. Big Sue is on duty till the evening and she won't worry if we're late."

"What about the afternoon gardening session with Uncle Bill? He'll definitely spot we're missing."

"Elementary, my dear Watson. You know how he loves his roses? Talks to them, probably takes them to bed with him. Well, I took a beauty from the nursery shop when no one was looking, last time we were in the village helping Uncle Dan with carrying the week's shopping. When I gave it to him he was well chuffed. Then I asked him if we could both miss gardening to go fishing."

"He didn't mind?"

"Not a chance – he was too busy stroking the rose I'd nicked. He'd have promised me anything!"

"So we're ready for the off?"

"3 days and counting."

Jonno was back in the Other Place. This time none of the Uncles was talking to him. This was very unusual. Instead he was in an unfamiliar landscape. Nothing was very clear. At first he thought he was in a school playground with dozens of youngish children noisily and busily chasing each other, skipping, whipping a spinning top, playing leap frog and throwing balls. A scene of delight so why did he feel increasingly uneasy? Then he realised with horror that the children, at first glance normal, all had monstrous deformed heads, grotesque faces, deep set eyes sunk in layers of wobbling flesh, protruding lipless mouths with razor teeth, no noses. It was the stuff of nightmares. At this point as he struggled for calm, it dawned on him that what he was seeing was a mix of two pictures he had recently studied in art class. He recalled the paintings vividly, one, he thought, was called "Children's Games" by a 16th or 17th Century Dutch artist. He was sure his name was Breughel. The other one was scary; something to do with a vision of the Underworld with nameless horrors like a giant fish with legs and it had a person's body sticking out of its mouth, eating him alive. He had shuddered as he looked at it and was certain that the artist was named Hieronymus Bosch. The visiting art lecturer had explained that the painter wished to emphasize what fate awaited those who were wicked. Jonno thought, "What I'm seeing is a sort of mixture of the two paintings. How horrible".

Uncle Jim's voice broke in on his thoughts. "You remember, metaphors, Jonathon?"

"Of course I do"

"What you're seeing is a metaphor."

Before Jonno could reply, Uncle said, "Come on, time for breakfast."

Jonno was unsettled. He picked without enthusiasm at his breakfast, eggs, ham and baked beans with crispy fried bread – normally one of his favourites. What was the significance of his confusion of the two paintings? He still felt shaken. The memory of the "children" who were not children was with him, powerfully. The Uncles had given it to him and they always had an agenda which was not always obvious. Did they know of his plans to leave Home with Bomber? Later, sitting in Maths, Jonno began to look more closely at the boys he thought he knew so well. He had already realised they were all hand picked by the Uncles for 2 reasons; they were all above average intelligence and they were all basically alone, without families or with families who had abandoned them. Now, he thought he could discern another, more startling factor. In the lunch hour, chatting with Bomber, Spike, Tom-Tom and a few others, he said. "You know, I've been wondering why the Uncles chose us and left the others."

"I'm just glad they did. Good grub, good company, good place – what more do you want?" answered Spike.

"There's something else, though."

"What?" This from Tom-Tom.

"Well, think about it. There are 25 of us and we're all especially good at one thing in particular as well as being fine all round."

"How do you mean?"

"For instance, you're bloody brilliant at anything to do with finding your way. You've got mental maps of everything in your head. You can work out where to go when there's no map and you've never been there before. That time we were competing against local school in night orienteering on the moor and it was foggy, you got us back to base in record time and every other team had to be rescued. Remember?"

Bomber answered instead, "I'd never thought about it before, but Jonno's right, Spike you're a mathematical genius, right? Haven't you been given a place at Cambridge and they want you as soon as possible. In fact, couldn't you go there in September this year even though you're only 15?"

"I could, yes, but I don't want to; and anyway the Uncles won't let me. They want me to go to the Big House with the rest of you, instead. Cambridge said they're holding the place for me, so it's OK by me."

"It's the same thing for quite a few of us. Don't forget, The Bug is going to Cambridge when he's 18, aren't you, Bugsy?"

"That's where you're wrong," replied the tall, thin boy with glasses, who already looked like a mad scientist to Jonno with his large glasses and long untidy hair.

"How – wrong?"

"I've told the Uncles I'm not going anywhere near Cambridge or any other university for that matter which tests on animals."

"Why not?"

"Too cruel. They're looking for cures for illnesses like Cancer and Parkinson's and Alzheimer's and they think they can do it by being cruel to animals."

"What do they do to them?"

"Hideous things. They wire them up with electrodes, they deliberately give them cancer and other things, they cut them up and—"

"O.K, I get the picture. But they are trying to find cures for all the illnesses, aren't they?"

"So what! Why should animals like cats, dogs, rabbits and monkeys suffer and die horribly, just for us? Anyway, they have the perfect answer – they don't need to use animals at all."

"What then?"

"Stuff called tissue culture, which is a substance that can be grown in dishes in the lab and, anyway, gives far more reliable results."

"Why don't the labs use it then?"

"Because most scientists don't give a damn about animals, they only want results and, of course, it's big business. All the horrible chemical companies like Smith, Kline and Beecham would complain to the government."

"What can you do?"

"I'm not sure yet, but I'm going to do something. For a start if Cambridge really wants me, and they seem to, they'll have to shut down their animal labs."

"Yes, but do they want you that much?"

"Certainly do. Remember, I won the Young Scientist of the Year last year. My project was on possible methods of saving bees and they liked it."

"Who liked it and why save bees?"

"The judges liked it. You must know about bees. They are dying out and that means disaster for crops, vegetable and fruit."

"Why?"

"Because bees pollinate everything, dickhead. Even you must know that. Without them, a lot of crops and plants would die out. Food would be hard to get. So if I can persuade the university that I can help and with other problems that are vital and if they really want me, they will use tissue culture instead of animals to test on."

"So the Uncles have chosen all of us for a particular skill we have," concluded Jonno, "and they are going to see us through university which will cost them a hell of a lot."

"So, we're lucky to be chosen by such good guys," said Tom-Tom. "Yes, but are they?"

"Who else would feed us, look after us, see us through uni? My family, if you could call it that, did nothing for me. They were glad to see the back of me."

"I know all that," replied Jonno, "I've got everything to thank them for too, but what really puzzles me is what they want in return?"

"How do you know they want something? I looked the Home up on the computer. It is listed as a charitable institution for disadvantaged boys, which sounds about right."

"Does it, though? Like I said before we are a select group of boys each with one outstanding gift which will get us into top universities and top jobs. We could, possibly be in positions of power, later on."

"I hope so. I might become governor of the Bank of England then

watch me save England's economy in a fortnight," laughed Spike.
"Of course you will," giggled Bomber, "and you'll give little hand-
outs to all your friends, won't you?"

"Or, perhaps, not so little," replied Spike, still amused by the idea.
At which point the bell sounded for Biology with their favoured
Mr Robson, bringing a slight whiff of fun and fireworks with him.
The day's topic, the digestive system, promised to be interesting and
possibly disgusting in Mr Robson's capable and experienced hands.
Jonno, Bomber and the others trooped happily into the biology lab.

Night. Returning to the Other Place, Jonno, still felt the slight
uneasiness which had never left him during the day. But things were
looking up for him. Uncle Jim was praising him for his essay on
'Lord of the Flies' and 'Animal Farm' in which he had to compare
them. The essay was entitled 'Man, a destructive influence'. He
had studied both for his O level English exam so knew them well.
"Excellent piece of work," enthused Uncle Jim, "As always, very
persuasive writing. Time for you to undertake some serious stuff –
politics perhaps".

"But I'm not very good at politics," objected Jonno, "I find P.P.E
lessons a bit boring. I like knowing what's going on outside here.
From what I can make out, this present government is full of weak
idiots and slimy back stabbers. I'd assassinate the lot."

"There are many ways to assassinate someone or something you
don't like, Jonno."

Jonno was surprised by Uncle Jim's response. He had expected at
least a mild reprimand for his outspoken comments. Instead, he
seemed to be taking them seriously.

""How do you mean?"

"Well, who can do the most damage to the government – and how?
Think about it."

"I suppose the press and T.V can spew out loads of poisonous
articles and programmes to rubbish them."

"There's your answer – the written and the spoken word. You remember that old chestnut – the pen is mightier than the sword?"

"What about it?"

"Come on, Jonathon. Surely you can see how powerful words are, fierce and deadly weapons in skilful hands."

"And?"

"You know very well what I mean. You have the ability with your words to persuade anyone to believe anything. Look at your writing for the House magazine. Remember how you talked everyone into dressing up as garden gnomes last Christmas and going round the town collecting money for Spike's animal charity?"

"Yeah. We collected shed loads of money. I was pleased for Spike. He was well chuffed."

"There you are, my point – the power of words. You will go far – Don't forget."

Uncle Jim was leaving. Jonno thought of his and Bomber's imminent departure. Suddenly the world outside the perimeter fence, the town in the far distance made the comfort of the Home very desirable. But – it was still a sort of prison, even though a pleasant one. Jonno knew he needed to explore that world. His resolve strengthened, he strolled by the quarry for a while, watching the swans and ducks busy with their young and a couple of irridescent dragon flies skeining the sunlight with their impossibly brilliant wings. He remembered Mr Robson telling them about pollution in the countryside, how agricultural chemicals were responsible for the drastic decline in butterflies and moths. Suddenly, watching the dragonflies, he started to compose a speech, an impassioned speech that he knew, with absolute certainty, he would deliver one day and many, many would listen.

Two days to countdown. I'm excited now, not even nervous. Can't wait to be free, out and about. Won't bother about taking loads of stuff, want to travel light, anyway. Must take rolled up sleeping bag, matches, comb. That's about it. Might take a few of the powdered food packets I took from the store room, some soup powder, dried milk, tea, sugar. That's the lot really. Divide it in backpacks between me and Bomber, should be pretty light. Hide it in the empty locker in our dorm. I reckon the main problem on Saturday night will be actually getting out of the house without being seen. Spike and Tom-Tom know we're thinking of leaving but they don't know when. And I don't want them to feel awkward. I know they wouldn't grass us up but if they don't see us go, they don't have to lie.

Friday. 1st lesson, games. Uncle Pete, games teacher is taking athletics practice for imminent sports day which they share with another school, a 'prestigious' private school (according to the glossy prospectus). St Andrews prides itself on its sports prowess and, with 230 boys as opposed to the Home's 25, is expected to take all trophies. However with Spike, an incredibly flexible high and long jump competitor and Bono, a future olympic style sprinter and member on an unbeaten relay team, the odds were fairly even. In fact, the two schools had both gained 6 trophies each last year.

The sun is shining brightly, but not too hotly. The scene is idyllic as boys run and jump and drink 7 up and lick ice lollies while the Uncles watch from the pavilion drinking tea. After lunch, as it's July and the summer holiday is about to begin, the boys are playing cricket and some of the Uncles join in.
Bomber and Jonno, waiting to bat, are lying in the long grass idly watching.
"Not long now."
"No, seems almost a shame to leave on such a good part of the year."
"Are you having second thoughts?"
"No, I'm really not. I'm looking forward to this – it's an adventure, Boys Own stuff."
"What stuff?"

"Oh, come on, Jonno – you must have heard of the Boys Own comic. Well, I think it was, back about a hundred years ago. Boys used to have adventures and it was always fun."

"What sort of adventures?"

"Discovering secret tunnels with treasure hidden there, villains who chased them and dangerous things happened to them – a bit like Indiana Jones, you know."

"Sounds fun. Do you think we'll discover any hidden tunnels or meet some villains?"

"I'd like the tunnels; not so sure about the villains. I don't mind Indiana Jones type villains; like German baddies who want the treasure or even James Bond's enemies who always want world domination but I don't want to meet the creepy types, like those weirdos we had to run away from. D'you remember that one they called Lanky Joe we saw just before we came here?"

"Don't! I still have nightmares about him."

That was the trouble with going to the Other Place. On the plus side there were plenty of fun things to do and old friends to meet, but reflected Jonno, there was a down side when someone you'd rather not see turned up out of the blue.

"C'mon, Jonno, our turn to bat. Stir your stumps! Get it, thicko – stir your stumps!"

Bomber is still creased with laughter at his own wit as Jonno aims a half-eaten apple in his direction.

Friday night. The boys had gone to bed later than the rest of the week. Thus usual routine is always more relaxed on Friday and Saturday evenings. The television stays on till around 10.30 and 'lights out' is more flexible. The dorm was finally quiet at around midnight as Jonno, tense under his duvet, decided to have a dummy run to see how easy – or not- it would be to leave the dorm unnoticed. He crept soundlessly to the door which was always left ajar and moved on to the landing. Subdued lighting showed him the stairs which led to the dark emptiness of the next two floors. He would not risk switching on any lights but had with him a pencil torch, which was almost too bright. He was surprised how tense he was and consciously tried to relax, moving downwards with the stealth of a cat.

He eventually reached the door to the outside and, after opening it very carefully, stepped into the night. The outlines of the rhododendron bushes were right in front of him and he understood at once why Billy, one of the boys who, in his former life, had earned money as a paper boy, delivering to 'posh' houses on the other side of the town where he grew up, often regaled the others with tales of his misadventures during the early morning and late evening rounds and told them the scariest part of his job was walking past rhododendron bushes on winter evenings.

"You never know what's behind them," he had observed darkly. Jonno wished he hadn't remembered this as, shivering a little in spite of the warmth of a July evening, he stood outside the door. As he stepped forward, he heard what sounded like a cat's purr but which rapidly became a deep throated nameless sound and a huge black shape hurtled by him. In his terror, to Jonno it seemed like a hunchback man with a huge head on massive shoulders with no neck. It stopped a few feet in front of him, bent down with its head swaying from side to side, making a hideous wet snuffling sound. Jonno moved back and still watching the Thing, edged inside the door and shut it firmly.

Returning swiftly to bed, Jonno reflected on what he'd seen, must be some sort of prowler, he reasoned but why? There was nothing of value in the Home. It hadn't seemed like a prowler, though, then what? More like a guard; guarding what? Of course, it must be there to stop anyone breaking out. Jonno came to a decision, he must tell Bomber about it and let him decide whether he still wanted to make their Great Escape. He was definitely going to try and hoped Bomber would be with him. Nevertheless, he must have a choice.

Bomber had no second thoughts. He still wanted to be part of the adventure. If anything, Jonno's account of what was now officially The Thing, only made him keener. Jonno could understand why Bomber's nick-name reflected his persona. Once committed to a course, he feared nothing, dared everything, the best to have on your side, a terrifying enemy.

Saturday at last. Breakfast, later at the weekend, more leisurely, no lessons, usually an outing or games against another school. On this particular Saturday, being the start of the summer holiday, the day was free of either and it promised endless sunshine and warmth. Everyone was in the swimming pond or basking lizard like on the sandy ground around the edge. Jonno, lazing chewing grass near the pond suddenly thought about all that he was wilfully leaving behind. What for some time had seemed an increasingly confined way of life, now felt almost cosy – almost but not quite. The swimming pond, a recent addition, was very attractive. The Uncles had managed to dig out a large area beside the wide and shallow stream that flowed through the grounds. Having diverted enough water into the newly formed pond they planted a myriad of water plants, Elodea, duck weed, yellow flag, bulrushes and introduced sticklebacks and minnow. Frogs and newts obligingly filled it with spawn and eggs. The pond was quite deep and wide and the Uncles seemed not to mind that the boys often took a dip. Jonno liked to swim gently among the plants on a summer evening while the fish softly ticked his toes.

Without warning, he was in the Other Place. Uncle Jim was sitting with him.

"Uncle, I've wondered for some time. Why do you do all this?"

"What are you referring to, Jonathan?"

"All this, you know, the house, the food, the teachers, everything. We were all living a rubbish life till you took us. What do you want back?"

"Do we have to want something back?"

"We've worked out that you were pretty selective who you chose to take off the streets."

"Absolutely correct, Jonathan. We are very particular. You have presumably also realised two things all 25 of you have in common?"

"We've all got one skill which we're very very good at."

"And the second?"

"We had all left home and most of us were homeless, living rough."

"So, you've answered your own question."

"Well, here's another. What is my skill?" What makes me so special? Bugsy is going to be, no, is already, a brilliant scientist, Spike could almost save the economy, now, at 15! What can I do to save the world?"

"You already know Jonathon, I told you precisely what you will do. You will change men's minds. More, you will move thousands with your rhetoric. No one will argue against you." His tone changed; there was warmth and a hint of laughter as he said,

"Aren't you pleased, Jonathan, to be in possession of a silver tongue? Soon, you will mature and you will possibly be capable of changing people's opinions, even telling them what to do"

"You mean I can play mind games with them?"

Uncle shrugged. "Call it what you will."

A strange sensation. He felt out of control for a few moments, then absolutely in control. The voice inside him said, "Don't think about it. Think about the pool, the fish, swimming in the moonlight, fish and chips," anything, he realised, except escaping.

Bomber's voice was beside him.

"Come on, Jonno, grub up. It's fish and chips and crumble and custard. We need to eat as much as poss to keep our energy levels up. Might be able to nick a bit of something to take with us."

Jonno shook his head vigorously to return to the pool and Summer Saturday. He jumped up.

"O.K. I'm with you; let's go."

After lunch, in the shade near the pool, Jonno, Bomber, Spike and Tom-Tom prepared for a session of their Cosine Game. The concept of this game belonged to Spike who had invented it during one particularly tedious Maths lesson when the Uncle had been explaining quadratic equations for the second time. The rules of the game had at first been simple. The Sines were evil beings from a parallel time zone in a mirror image universe who were continually at war with the morally upright Cosines. On a handmade board, similar to a chess board, the two sides fought to capture the Tower at the centre, using the throw of the dice to win or lose ground. Somehow, though, neither side ever triumphed. It was always a stand-off, both of them waiting for a chink in the other's armour. Gradually the rules grew more complex. Like chess, the game became cerebral. The dice were abandoned, strategy and psychological warfare were all-important. Bomber, being considered most artistic, had prepared a large and detailed board, complete with ambushes, tunnels, steel traps, hidden dangers, mires, covered pits, deadly snakes and sudden terrors, invented by anyone of the boys on the spur of the moment. These new dangers would throw the others into disarray and thus make the whole game more interesting. Also the boundaries between the goodies and the baddies became blurred and, after several games, the Sines were sometimes quite nice, the Cosines sometimes a bit nasty.

They did not always look the same. For one week's play they might be human in appearance but not necessarily in behaviour. Then one of the four boys would turn them into aliens. Tom-Tom's reconstructed Sines and Cosines were usually the most imaginative and complex creatures.

"You're going to miss this," warned a voice in Jonno's head. He was annoyed by this reminder and tried to change the subject, focussing instead on what food to sneak furtively out of the dining room at teatime. As it turned out he had no need to be furtive as only two Uncles were in the dining hall and they were deep in conversation.

The rest of the Uncles were away for the weekend at least, while some would be absent for a fortnight. Jonno, Bomber and some of the other boys were intrigued by their absence, trying to guess where they went. They appeared to have no families or friends. They had no visitors and apparently no interest outside the Home. In fact, Jonno thought they took very little notice of each other and even their contact with the boys was confined to the class room and their progress. Strangely enough though, when Jonno was in the Other Place at night, he frequently met the Uncles, had conversations with the revision of the previous day's lesson topics and, occasionally, general discussions. He sometimes felt he knew the Uncles better from the conversations in the Other Place rather than in the day time. This fact worried him or rather nagged at the back of his mind, an irritation that would not go away.

However, Jonno had plenty to think about. "Tonight's the night. Should be easy for us to get away unnoticed, Bomber," he said as they ate peanut butter sandwiches and chocolate sponge. In the Uncle's absence, Big Sue had given all the boys a bottle of coca cola, a treat they greatly appreciated.

"Just think, we'll be able to drink this whenever we want," mused Bomber as he wrapped some sandwiches and cake in paper and put a banana and an apple in separate pockets.

"Too right."

"I reckon we'll miss being waited on, though. We've gone soft while we've been here, we'll never be able to survive on the streets."

"We won't need to. As soon as we're out of the perimeter, we'll hide till first light them hitch our way East towards Devon, Dorset and then Somerset and Sussex." All this sounded rather vague to Bomber, who was relieved Tom-Tom had drawn a map for them. He also knew that he would stand a better chance of following it than Jonno whose map reading skills had been shown as less than perfect on the last orienteering weekend.

"Another thing, Bomber. No one will give us a second look."

These days we look like any kid who's on holiday or exploring somewhere. Don't forget we'll be wearing normal clothes, proper haircut and all that. In fact, our old friends in London would never recognise us. We look like right poshos."

Ten thirty and most boys were either in bed or getting ready for bed. Jonno had made sure that he had casually reminded the others in the dorm that he and Bomber were going on an early morning fishing trip and would probably miss the Gardening Session. As it turned out, Uncle cancelled it anyway so that gave them even longer before anyone wondered where they were.

Jonno and Bomber, tense and fully dressed under their covers, waited for everyone to fall asleep. They had placed their backpacks in the cupboard in the toilets outside the dormitory. Finally, at around 11.30 Jonno judged it was safe to leave. Everywhere was silent. They left the dorm, crept soundlessly down the stairs after picking up the backpacks. Out of the door near the gym and into the silence of a hazy moonlit July night. The moon, low in the sky, glowed like a piece of Edam cheese, just bright enough to show them the shadowy path between bushes before the running track and the fence. Jonno had managed to find some wire cutters in the shed and they were safely in his rucksack. Bomber, suddenly tense as they stood outside the door getting their bearings, whispered, "What's that over there?"

"There's something moving between those two bushes."

"I can't see anything."

Bomber remembered his fear out here when he'd come out before to check everything.

"I think it could be something guarding the place," his voice hardly reaching Jonno. "We'll just have to make a run for it."

This was an unappealing decision to Jonno, but it was that or go back, so, taking a deep breath, he said. "Ready when you are."

But Bomber froze. The bush that wasn't a bush moved again.

The movement was decisive and threatening. Something large was coming towards them. Bomber could not make out any definite shape but it looked as if small sharp glints of light were switched on and off in the deeper than dark darkness. Bomber clutched Jonno.

"What's that?" he croaked like a frog.

"What's what?"

Bomber couldn't reply. The darkness was around him, the outlines of the trees and bushes were no longer there. He was somewhere else where he didn't want to be. Then something was pulling at him and a voice was calling him from a long way away.

"Bomber! Bomber, what's up with you? Stop messing about or it'll be daylight."

Jonno stood impatiently in the fitful moonlight.

"Didn't you see it?"

"What?"

"That shape with the eye things in it?"

"Where?"

"Here. It was all round us. You must have seen it."

"I didn't see a thing. You must be going barmy. Stop messing about. We're making for the track over, right?"

Jonno's obvious lack of fear calmed Bomber slightly, so, still shaking, he followed his friend across the grass to the track. Once there, they quickly found the blind spot which Bomber had identified before and Jonno set about cutting a hole in the perimeter fence.

"Are you going to help or just stand there looking gormless?"

Bomber blinked. The shape faded; he crouched to help Jonno. Already a fairly large hole had appeared. Soon Jonno put down the cutters and they were through. The world was silent. Bomber felt light headed and he wondered uneasily if they were enveloped in the Blackness again, then gradually he began to discern hills gleaming pale in the come-and-go moonlight.

"Come on, move it. We've got to get as far as possible before tomorrow."

"Which way?"

"I looked at Tom-Tom's maps this evening. We need to get far from Cornwall very quickly. We'll find a road and hitch a lift if we can. Otherwise we'll get on a train as far as Exeter or farther. There's a load of little stations between Penzance and Exeter where it would be piss easy to sneak on a train. Come on, this way."

Chapter 2. Escape to Danger

Jonno led the way up a farm track between high hedges. Already, in July, there were chunky balls of harvested wheat on one side of the track. Somewhere water sounded and elsewhere something shrieked. Everything was raw and strange. Bomber thought of the Home. Then a farm building was near, big and looming, scufflings inside. "Creep past. There might be dogs."

Yes, thought Bomber, and they will be big with red eyes and slavering chops.

Past the barn. No dogs. More farm buildings, full of eyes. Through the yard, past the farmhouse itself, on to a quiet road. They set out on what Jonno hoped was the way out of Cornwall. He was suddenly elated, free as he had been a long time ago in the orchard at Runcton, sitting in an apple tree while the chickens moved in the long grass below him. Bomber, too, had relaxed and he began to share some of Jonno's excitement. His heart seemed to be very busy. It was jumping about all over the place as if it had broken free from its moorings. He took a deep breath, held it, counted to ten slowly then released it. They walked on. After about a mile, the road ended in a small square, surrounded by some five or six stone cottages of various sizes and a longer single storey wooden building which, when they moved closer, they saw had a notice saying 'Melylen Village hall'.

"Not much of a village", whispered Jonno, "Looks like a dead end."

"There's a path over there", said Bomber. "It's going in the right direction."

The path was about 6 feet wide and, by the hard smoothness of the earth, appeared well trodden by many feet. There were trees with smooth trunks, evenly spaced on either side which gave it the impression of being a processional way. Bomber felt this almost immediately and wondered where the path would take them. Somewhere very important, he thought, and could be dangerous. Jonno was similarly affected by the feeling of awe, but this excited

35

him and he moved faster. They walked for ages, they thought. The path was fairly straight, the trees leading to a vanishing point in the gloom ahead. Already there was a hint of lightness in the eastern sky. The end of the path was abrupt. Without warning the trees ended in a small square, surrounded by an ancient wall, crumbling and with plants growing from it. In the centre was a well, overgrown but with the glint of water. A small tree grew by the side of the well and, at first, Bomber couldn't work out why the outline looked odd, until he realised that the branches were covered with pieces of cloth. As the sky lightened he could see that the materials ranged from delicate gossamer and lace to pieces of torn hessian, even socks and scarves. "How weird," remarked Jonno. "They must have walked miles to put them here. What's it all in aid of?"

"I reckon it's some sort of offering. Somehow I don't want to hang around here. Look, we can get into that field and climb over that hill. I bet there's a road on the other side. Come on, let's go."

By the time they reached the top of the slight hill, it was early dawn and already a mildness was in the air. No road but another field with huge stones in front of them.

"Look, a mini Stonehenge!" said Jonno "let's go down and have something to eat. I'm starving."

Hurtling down with Bomber, Jonno felt the same happiness he had felt earlier. They entered the circle, feeling the hardness and age of the stones, most of them still fairly upright, a few leaning or fallen in the long grass, which was whipping round the boys' ankles in the lively dawn wind. They leaned against the largest and wolfed down the cheese sandwiches they had made at tea the day before and ate the apples they had scrumped from an overhanging tree in the tiny hamlet which they had found.

"This is good stuff. Now we need to push on, find a road and see if we can hitch a lift – as long as it's going upwards and not back down towards Penzance."

But Bomber did not answer. He was elsewhere. The stone was warm, it was breathing. He could feel its heart – or –something moving beneath his hands as he touched it. The stone spoke to him without words he could recognise but he knew what they meant. Stay Stay. It was a command, not a request. Out there you will fail. It was a threat, not a warning. There was the throbbing of a drum in the stone and he was part of it. Suddenly Uncle Jim was in his head, speaking to him – menacing, not his usual self at all. Bomber couldn't decipher what he was saying –

"Bomber, what's up with you? What the hell are you playing at?" Jonno was pulling at him, trying to loosen his grip on the stone. Finally, Jonno prized his hands from the stone. His palms were scratched and bleeding. Jonno was staring at him, worried and puzzled. Bomber was still unsure where he was. He still felt part of the stone circle. He didn't want to leave but he knew he must.

"I can't tell you what was happening, I don't know myself. I was part of the stone circle – it was alive and wanted me to do something."

"What?"

"I don't know. Let's get away, quickly. Let's find the road."

They ran through the circle, over a stile and were on a roadside by another quiet road but wider this time with road markings. As they stood uncertainly a van came into view. Quickly Jonno stepped forward and held up his hand as if to hail a bus. The van stopped. Written on the side in large letters were the words 'Tregarron's Veg and Fruit'.

"What's up? D'you want a lift?"

"Please. Are you going towards Exeter?"

"Not that far, but on the way. Will that do?"

"Yes, thanks."

They climbed in beside him. He seemed very pleasant and, to their relief, he didn't ask questions about what they were doing or who they were. Afterwards they realised that this was odd but at the time they were simply pleased. The driver was, he explained, delivering produce to a village shop further on, then would return to his farm near Penzance. He left them by a small railway station named Lostwithiel. It was some distance from the town since there was nothing around it and no people either.

"Doesn't look as if any trains come here."

"I know but they must do. Here's a current timetable. Look, they actually go to London."

"But we don't want to go to London."

"I know that, idiot. We're aiming for Sussex. But we've got to get away from here, in case the police are after us."

"D'you reckon the Uncles will get the fuzz on to us?"

"Probably. How else would they get us?"

"So you think they'll be after us?"

"You bet. They haven't spent all that money on us just to let us escape. You must see that. I reckon we're being prepared for something important."

"Such as?"

"I wish I knew. Whatever it is, they've kept it under wraps. There's only one thing I found out and that was by accident."

"Tell me."

"Well, d'you remember a boy called Justin Whiteley, who came to give us a lecture about trying to get into a good university. He'd been at our Home, gone to Uni. Later. I asked him what his work was but he didn't really say, just said he'd got a really good position in a law firm. I thought that was very vague then later, I overheard him talking to a few of the Uncles in the staff room. The door was ajar and I was outside. One of the Uncles, I don't know which one, said to him, "Have you infiltrated the Inner Sanctum yet? Have you put the message across yet?" And he said "Oh yes, no problem in that direction. I've got them eating out of my hand!" And the Uncle said something and they all laughed".

"It all sounds a bit creepy. I'd like to know what's really going on".

"So would I. Maybe we can find out."

"How?"

"I'm not sure but we're in a better position to find out if we're on the outside."

"I don't see how."

"Neither do I, exactly, but we can at least try to discover what they are up to. It'll be playing detectives."

"Who'll we get to help us?"

"Well, that's why I'm aiming to get to Sussex to Runcton where Auntie and Uncle live. They will help us, I know."

"Not another Uncle!"

"Not one of those. Uncle Tom is great. He'll know what to do."

"We've got to get there first. Are we going to sneak on a train somehow?"

By now, it was 7.30 and life was beginning to stir in and around the station. Jonno considered. He could see very few station staff. In fact, most people arriving at the station seemed to have season tickets as they went straight on to the platform. He decided the best plan was to do the same, especially as there was no one looking at tickets.

"Come on," he said, "It's now or never. Look relaxed and we'll go straight on to the platform and get on the next train going up the line."

They walked on to the right platform and in minutes the London train arrived. It was already crowded, which was a good thing as they could mingle with everyone else and hopefully avoid unwanted attention. So far so good, thought Jonno, no one's staring at us. He was wrong. Bomber said quietly, "I don't like the way that bloke over there keeps glancing at us from behind his paper. Don't look now. I'll tell you when. A pause. "Now."

Jonno looked across the aisle. Obliquely across from them, 4 men sat at a table, 2 reading papers, 2 playing chess on a small board. All 4 appeared engrossed, until suddenly one of the men glanced across at the boys and as quickly glanced away. It was almost subliminal thought Bomber like subliminal advertising on television which he had read about and been vastly intrigued by the concept.

The man was definitely interested in them. He seemed immersed in his paper but Bomber noticed that he never turned the page as the other reader did. The chess players were silent, apparently absorbed in their game, but Bomber felt the whole group were acting in a play or in a tableau. He was growing uneasy, when Jonno whispered, "There's a ticket inspector, we'll have to move." They made their way, as casually as possible down the coach away from the approaching ticket inspector until they reached a toilet.
"Quick, in here," said Jonno.
Squashed in the small space, hardly breathing, they waited. After a while, when nothing happened, they emerged with caution and went the opposite way until they found 2 free seats together. This time no one took any notice of them at all.
"We'll get off at Exeter," decided Jonno. "We'll hitch towards Devon and Dorset or Wiltshire."
This sounded somewhat imprecise to Bomber but he wasn't worried as he knew they had tom-Tom's intriguing maps to help them.
"O.K. Whatever," replied Bomber. "I didn't like the look of that bloke who kept looking at us. He was definitely interested in us."
"I think you imagined it. I didn't notice him looking at us. In any case, he can't know who we are and we don't look suspicious. We're not scruffy. With these rucksacks, we just look as if we're on holiday."
"Well, I hope we don't see him again. What do you reckon they'll do when they find we've gone? Will they get the police on to us?"
"They might, but somehow I think they'll look for us themselves. I don't know why I think this; I've got a suspicion the Uncles have a sort of secret network of spies who can find out anything."
"Yeah, I think so, too. Where do you think they are?"
"Everywhere."
"So the scary bloke back there could be one of them?"
"I don't think so. They can only just have found out that we've gone."

"I'm not so sure. Funny things have been happening to me, anyway, since we left."

"How do you mean?" asked Jonno.

"I didn't say anything before because it sounded stupid, crazy. When we went into the garden last night, I thought I saw a huge shapeless thing coming towards me. It covered me and I couldn't see anything. I thought I was in a different place a long way off. It was horrible."

"I remember you standing there looking vacant," said Jonno, "But I didn't see anything."

"Then when we crossed into that stone circle I felt really strange as if the stones were alive and I was part of them. It was like I was living a long time ago and I wanted to stay there. I belonged there. What do you think it means, Jonno?"

"I'm not sure, Bomber. You've always been a bit different, haven't you? Let's face it – you always used to scare us pooless when we first came to the Home. At night you said there were strange eyes looking at us and once you even said there was a figure in white standing in the middle of the dorm. You really terrified us with your stories."

"They weren't made up stories. I really did see things. I'm not kidding you. After a while they stopped."

Before Jonno could reply, the train slowed and he realised the announcer had said something about Exeter. Looking out of the window he could see they were arriving at a large town with endless rows of terraced houses and busy intersecting roads.

"Come on, this must be Exeter."

The train slowed to a halt. They left the train, trying to look as casual as possible, went past the ticket collector without difficulty. He was occupied with two passengers who had shown him a map and were clearly asking for directions. Once out of the station they saw a bus pulling up at a bus stop. It was already crowded which Jonno considered was what they needed – lots of people made them much less likely to be noticed. As the bus pulled away with the boys sitting on the top deck, Bomber thought he glimpsed the staring man on the train. He was standing at the bus stop looking at the bus. He said nothing to Jonno, however. The bus travelled through a remote and beautiful landscape, pulling up at isolated clusters or houses where five or six people would leave. Jonno and Bomber relaxed and soon dozed, both being fairly tired. This was not surprising, thought Jonno sleepily, since they had been awake for over 30 hours already. They were awoken by the bus driver reminding them it was Moonbury, the stop they had requested.

As the bus pulled away, they took stock of their surroundings. Moonbury seemed to be two or three farm buildings, a small farm house and lots of cows. A van appeared from the direction they had come. Impulsively, Jonno stepped forward, and raised his hand as if hailing a bus. The van stopped. The driver, his face in shadow, wound down the window.

"What's up?"

"Can you give us a lift, please?"

There was a brief silence, then "O.K. Get in. I can take you as far as the outskirts of Dorchester. I'm going to a farm up that way. Will that do?"

"Yes, please. That'd be brilliant."

They climbed in and sat by him, with Jonno in the middle. He glanced surreptitiously at the driver. He was staring straight ahead. Jonno noticed two things about the man which worried him. One, he was clutching the steering wheel very tightly indeed, his knuckles stretched white. Two, he seemed to have a nervous tic, grimacing at regular intervals, the left side of his face pulled taut, exposing uneven stained teeth. "I don't like this", thought Jonno, "we'll have to get off, somehow." He sensed Bomber's tenseness next to him and knew that he had seen it, too. Jonno tried to think of an escape plan.

The driver, who had hitherto remained silent, suddenly spoke, "Where are you two going?"

"Oh, just to visit a relative of mine," improvised Jonno.

"Where exactly?"

Silence. Then, "Crewkerne", he replied, having seen it on the side of a passing van.

"Whereabouts? I know Crewkerne well."

"In the High Street." Jonno was becoming desperate. He hoped that Crewkerne had a High Street. He reasoned that most placed do.

"Where have you come from?"

"From my home just outside Exeter," Bomber said quickly.

"Where's that?"

Bomber made up an address and hoped that this particularly inquisitive driver did not know every road in Crewkerne, and on the outskirts of Exeter. Both Jonno and Bomber felt increasingly uneasy in the van and wanted to escape. Easier said than done. The driver was very interested in them, firing questions at them until they became confused and even Bomber was finding if difficult to invent further names and addresses. Also, the nervous tic was quite frightening and reminded Bomber of a particular hideous gargoyle on the church roof near the Home.

"Actually, this would do. Could you put us down here, please," asked Jonno.

"This is nowhere near Dorchester where I'm heading or Crewkerne where you say you're going, so why do you want to get off?"

For a start the boys didn't like the way he said, "where you say you're going," as if he was perfectly aware they were lying. Nor did they want to be interrogated any further. The driver was showing far too much interest in them. Most of all they needed to run away from the Gargoyle, himself. When the van slowed almost to a standstill at a junction, Bomber stealthily tried the door handle. It was securely locked. They were imprisoned. A little further on there was a queue building up on the road ahead and the Gargoyle wound down his window to speak to a workman on the other side of the road. Bomber whispered to Jonno, "He's locked the door, somehow we've got to get out."

"How?"

"I'm thinking." He had seen which switch operated the central locking system though he was pretty sure the Gargoyle didn't realise Bomber had seen him therefore if his attention was elsewhere momentarily Bomber could de-activate the central locking and he and Jonno could escape. This plan, of course, was dependent on two factors; one that the van was slowing and, two, that he could convey his plan to Jonno, unheard. Factor two turned out to be easily done. Another junction, the driver in front of their van was proceeding very cautiously. This annoyed the Gargoyle who opened his window and shouted angrily at the offending car. Bomber quickly whispered the plan to Jonno who nodded to signify agreement. So far so good. Now it was vital for Jonno to have an opportunity to reach across to the appropriate switch. The van drove on, it seemed for hours. The Gargoyle was clearly avoiding built up areas. They passed through no towns, hardly any villages. Instead, the quiet lane wound between hedges of frothy cow parsley, deep coombes and wooded valleys and crossed shallow, fast running streams. Jonno began to feel they would drive forever when, unexpectedly, an opportunity arose. Ahead of them in the lane, a herd of cows was slowly crossing the lane. Infront of the van a car had stopped. The herdsman who was watching the cows apparently knew the car driver and was chatting to him. The Gargoyle drummed his hands on the wheel, impatient. He wound his window down, Jonno leant across, unlocked the doors, Bomber opened his side, jumped out. Jonno followed, slammed the door shut and they were gone. Aware of shouting behind them, they hared down an overgrown footpath a little way behind where the van had stopped. Soon there was only the sound of a distant tractor and birdsong in the hedges of the ubiquitous cow parsley mixed with all the other wild flowers of an abundant July. At last, breathless, they slowed to a walk and listened. Still only birdsong, now mixed with faraway farm sounds and sheep talking to one another behind a nearby hedge.

"That was close, Jonno."

"You're not joking. I wonder where he was going to take us".

"Somewhere we didn't want to go, I guess. Do you think he's sussed out who we were?"

"I can't see how he could have, but I didn't want to find out. He made the hair on the back of my neck stand up."

"He was pretty scary with that horrible way his mouth curled up on one side. I reckon he's a weirdo."

"No kidding. No more hitching, agreed? From now on we'll go by train. Seemed easy enough to Exeter."

"Definitely, no more hitching. We'll walk for a while till we know where we are then we'll look at Tom-Tom's maps, and plan something. Let's have something to eat, I'm starving."

They still had plenty of dried ready meals which were used for night orienteering outings. They also had one bottle of water each of which they used part to rehydrate the powdered vegetable soup and dried potato. It was still rather powdery but they were too hungry to mind. They accompanied the meal with the last of the bread they'd taken the previous evening from the dining hall.

When they'd finished, they sat on the edge of a little stream they'd found and paddled their feel in the cold, clear water, watching tiny transparent fish darting like arrows around their toes. They both felt impossibly happy at that moment, as if nothing could touch them and only good things lay ahead.

Chapter 3. The Mysterious Manor

Jonno looked at his watch. Six o'clock. "We'd better carry on, look for a barn or something to sleep in tonight."

"Yes, but first let's find a signpost to find out where exactly we are." They began following a fairly well defined footpath across a field, which led through two more fields, past some shady woodland where oak trees dappled the edge of the wood with moving shadows and sunlight. The path then climbed a hill from which they could see more fields and woodland and also some turrets behind trees which looked mysterious and attractive to Jonno and Bomber.

"Looks like Sleeping Beauty's castle," said Jonno.

"Let's break in and rescue her," laughed Bomber, "but don't forget we'll have to cut down a hundred year's growth of brambles."

"She'll probably be disappointed when she sees us. She's been expecting a handsome prince, don't forget."

They carried on across country in the general direction of what they guessed was a manor house set in vast grounds of lawns and woodland. After some time they came to an avenue of trees on either side of an over grown grassy wide path.

"This looks as if it was once a driveway to a big house, don't you think?" asked Jonno. Before Bomber could reply, they suddenly heard faint music coming from somewhere ahead of them. It was very pleasant music; they wanted to see where it came from. They walked, without talking, down the green way. The music was enticing and drew them on. There were voices singing, sweet voices. They had to see who it was. Suddenly, round a bend in the drive, they came, amazed, to a sudden halt. In front of them was a vast garden with the turreted house in the background. The lawn was covered with heaps of white flowers and blossom, stirring gently in the slight early evening breeze. A large table with a white tablecloth was heaped with food, dishes of bright fruit, every fruit you could think of, cakes of myriad types with delicate icing and design, heaped and lucent jellies, wonderful chocolate creations, dark and light, all set inside a white and gold pavilion, draped with looped curtains of a gossamer material.

The music came from a group of four young boys of about 16 – 18 years who sat on a raised bandstand, circular with a roof and supporting poles, which were covered with vines, ribbons and paper lanterns. One boy played what looked like a small piano but wasn't. A second boy had a sort of violin, another played a flute and the fourth played a harp. What really caught the two boys' attention were the young girls, lots of them, all about 15 or 16 years old and all dancing to the music. They wore bright dresses, of rainbow colours and to Bomber they seemed like butterflies fluttering jewel like over the lawn.

The two boys stood astonished. One of the dancers suddenly saw them.

"Hi", she called, coming towards them, "we've been waiting for you. Come on, have something to eat, then you must dance with us". She stood in front of Jonno and Bomber and they saw she was accompanied by a huge black dog, slim but muscular who stood pressed to her side. "I'm Maisie and this is Prince." She looked, thought Jonno, like a being from another time and place who might suddenly disappear when the clock struck twelve. However, her laughter was bright and her touch real as she took his hand firmly and led him to the pavilion or marquee, Jonno wasn't sure which, where the trestle table was heaped with food. Bomber followed, speechless like his friend. The music changed to a slower, quieter tune as the dancers stopped and drifted towards the boys and Maisie. They stood in a circle around them, chattering and laughing happily. Jonno was surrounded by about five girls who were showing him something which shone gold in the lowering sunlight. Bomber, thought Jonno, as he glanced across at him standing with Maisie and Prince, seemed dazed and his eyes were fixed on Maisie's vivid, excited face.

"We were hoping you wouldn't be late," said one of the girls to

Jonno. "When we've eaten, we are going to play hide and seek, then
more dancing before we swim in the pool in lantern light." Jonno
wondered how the girls knew they would arrive at the manor and,
if he hadn't been nearly as entranced as his friend, he might have
been very worried indeed. Soon they were hungrily devouring the
delicious tasting food and drink as they listened to the animated
conversations around them. Afterwards neither Jonno nor Bomber
could recall what food they ate and what the girls said remained
a skein of bright words, an abstract pattern they could nearly
remember but not quite. Except for Maisie, Jonno could remember
everything about her everything they talked about. She deflected his
question when he asked her how the girls knew of their imminent
arrival.

"Oh, we knew about it. Don't worry and I shall see you again,
anyway."

"Where, when?" said Jonno, puzzled.

"At uni, of course, you know we will." And suddenly, he did know,
very clearly and very definitely. He was walking along a towpath
on a moonlit December evening holding Maisie's hand in a city
he recognised although he couldn't name it, yet. Prince walked by
Maisie's side.

"Yes I do know, I'm stupid, I've know all the time. Let's hurry up and
play hide and seek. I want to explore this place."

The game began. By now the sun was low in the sky and shadows
were long across the lawns. Bomber stayed with Maisie and Jonno
for a while then set off by himself to explore the grounds and the
manor itself. The catcher, a girl with long, dark hair in two glossy
plaits, warned them all she would find them all wherever they hid.
The band was still playing softly as Bomber entered the house. He
knew what he would see and for some reason this did not surprise
him. He must find the answer and find it quickly why this was. He
climbed the wide baronial staircase. On the first bend stood a suit
of shining armour, 6 feet tall, with the right arm raised as if to strike.

Bomber moved uneasily past, wondering if the suit was occupied. He seemed to be alone on the upper gallery where more knights stood guard outside heavily curtained doors. He could hear excited shrieks mingled with music and laughter, but distantly. No sign of the Catcher so Bomber relaxed his guard and curiosity made him open one of the metal studded heavy oak doors. It opened easily to his hesitant touch and, at the same instant, he knew how amazing the room would be and this knowledge frightened him more than anything else. It superceded the meeting with Maisie, the magical party, the amazing house. Although he knew he had never ever been in this part of the country before, let alone to this house and he had never met Maisie, or the girls, nevertheless he realised with absolute certainty that somehow he knew some things about his life as if he could look into a crystal ball. He couldn't see everything. He couldn't see what the Uncles really were up to or, for that matter, who they were. He also clearly wanted to know if they were following them secretly or had informed the police of their escape.

Meanwhile he stood in the room and, in spite of his current worries, was lost in admiration at the splendour in front of him. The room was large and high ceilinged with a huge uncurtained bay window. Almost filling the room was a giant telescope facing the window. It was exactly the same as the one Bomber had seen at a Science museum which had an adjoining observatory. The only other thing in the room was a small table containing instruments which Bomber thought must be connected with the telescope. He was about to step on to the platform to see if he could use it when he heard voices drawing nearer. Going quickly to the door, he looked both ways cautiously, saw no one, moved into the long gallery with the knights and hid behind a curtain where he could see without being seen. For a while nothing, then footsteps approaching, determined footsteps, doors being opened. The Catcher? Bomber peered round cautiously, then drew back fearfully. Two men were walking purposefully down the gallery away from him, sometimes opening doors.

He stood, trembling till they turned a corner then slipped away in the opposite direction.

The game of hide and seek took on a new urgency. The new Catchers were not fun. They were not laughing and they were seeking him and Jonno. He knew this and danger was all about them. "I've got to find Jonno," he thought. "He probably won't have seen them. He could be anywhere." He decided to ask for help from one of the band. He could hear them still. Dusk was nearly there and the lanterns were alight and fluttering in the trees and on the bandstand. Bomber peered out of a window on the ground floor. No sign of the two men. He ran fast across the lawn to the four boys who had now stopped playing except for the boy at the piano type instrument who was playing a soft lulling tune. "Please, will you help me?" The desperation in his voice was obvious. The boy stopped and they all focussed on Bomber.

"What's up?", said the boy with the flute, "why aren't you playing the hide and seek game?"

"I am", answered Bomber, "but there are two men after me and my friend, Jonno and it's not a game. I'll explain later, but can you help us, please. I need to find Jonno so that we can get away fast."

The band were keen to help and saw it as a challenge. The boy with the flute thought for a moment then said, "you sit here with my flute. I'll look for your friend. When I find him, I'll hide him in the cellar, then I'll come back for you. Can you play the flute?" he added hopefully.

"Not a chance", answered Bomber with regret.

"Just pretend, then. You others play so it looks normal. I'll be as quick as I can."

He walked off and disappeared across the lawn, helped by the dying light and the shadows. Bomber tried to relax and look as if he knew how to play the flute. Girls flitted across the lawn, voices high with excitement, sometimes with the Catcher in hot pursuit. Bomber suddenly became aware of two figures walking near the bandstand and they were not talking. The two men glanced at the band, then looked again. Bomber was sweating with fear; trying to look unconcerned as he held the flute, shaking, to his lips, not daring to breathe in case he inadvertently blew it and sounded a discordant note. The men stared harder. At this crucial point the girl Catcher saved the day. She emerged from the gloom, shouting to the band, "Have you seen the boys? I really want to catch them."

The boy with the harp, quick as a flash, answered, "You're in luck. They've just not long gone past. I heard them say they were going to hide in the old Summerhouse by the weir."

"Thanks, see you."

"No, wait a minute. Let them think they've won. After a while we'll all come with you and surprise them."

"O.K," she agreed, "I don't fancy going down there by myself in the dark. It's a bit spooky."

She sat down with the band as the two sinister Catchers walked quickly in the direction of the Summerhouse. The band moved fast. The harpist quickly told the astonished Catcher what was going on, the piano player set off to help search for Jonno. He soon returned with the real flute player and the news that Jonno had been found, was safely in the cellar and they were ready to escort Bomber there, too. Bomber and the band entered the outside door to the kitchen, went down the stairs and found Jonno with some of the girls sitting on barrels in the vast underground room. The manor must once have served a very wealthy establishment of master and family plus a host of servants. Now it smelt musty and there were rustlings and scampering's in the dark corners. Light came faintly from four slits high up in the wall. Maisie was there with the other girls. Prince lay by the door, head and ears raised on guard.

"Who are those men?" asked Maisie.

"We don't know," said Jonno. "They could be police, but I think it's more likely they could be sent by the Uncles at our Home."

"Probably," agreed Bomber. "I don't know how they managed it, but we seem to have been watched and followed from the minute we got away."

Maisie and the rest of the girls knew the boys' story and were keen to help.

"When they don't find us at the Summerhouse they'll keep looking," Jonno pointed out.

"Don't worry," said Maisie, "I've had an idea. Listen. What if Robert and Peter pretend to be you two and lead them away from here?" Robert and Peter were two members of the band, the harpist and flute player. They were happy to agree to the plan, looking on it as a great adventure. On Maisie's advice, they exchanged top clothes to help deceive the two unknown Catchers. The two were then going to loudly discuss their intention of going to the nearest railway station to catch a train to London when they knew the men had seen them. As it was now dark, they all agreed to have some supper, go to bed and put the plan into operation early next morning. Bomber and Jonno were exhausted after so much excitement and no sleep for a long time. After a delicious supper which the girls seemed to prepare out of nowhere and in no time at all, Jonno and Bomber sleepily listened as the girls and the band talked lazily in the vast living room or hall of the manor house. Huge windows gave on to the lawns, where paper lanterns still shone with subdued radiance in the trees and in the pavilion. The room had many chairs and sofas piled high with soft cushions. Soon, Jonno and Bomber drifted into sleep, so deep that no voices or thoughts came to them from the Other Place.

They awoke to the strident sound of a peacock on the lawn outside the window. The sun was high. Jonno looked at his watch. He leapt up from the sofa he had been lying on.

"It's 11 o'clock," he told Bomber, "but where is everyone?" He went to the door which led to a corridor, which in turn went to the large kitchen they'd eaten in the night before. Bomber followed. It was empty, not only of people but also of the dishes, cups, plates and food which had been piled up the night before. Silence. No girls, no band, no lanterns, no coloured ribbons, no pavilion. The house, they could tell, was empty. No chairs, no cushions, the magnificent staircase uncarpeted.

"This place has been empty for ages," exclaimed Jonno. "What the hell? Did we dream it all?"

"Only if we both had the same dream," said Bomber. "Anyway, look at that," he said suddenly, pointing at the ground. In front of them lay a flute; the same flute bomber had held the day before, unmistakably the same, with the same letters "PETER" in marker ink written clearly on it. Jonno quickly ran up the main staircase to look for clues. There were none. The rooms upstairs were empty, completely empty. He glanced in the room which Bomber had told him about. The telescope was no longer there. He returned to Bomber. "Nothing," he said, then, "But what's that?"

An envelope lay on a small table near the sofa where Bomber had fallen asleep. Bomber picked it up. He handed it to Jonno. "It's addressed to you," he said.

Jonno took it, puzzled. His name, in clear italic handwriting was written on the blue envelope. He opened it. Inside was a thin silver chain with a circular pendant carved into an interleaved pattern. He recognised it at once. Maisie had been wearing it. He held it carefully, gently replaced it in the envelope and placed it in the inside pocket of his trousers, or rather the trousers he'd swapped the previous night. Both boys felt a sudden and deep yearning for their companions of that night. Jonno said, after a few moments, "They've saved our bacon, I reckon. Robert and Peter must've pulled it off. Those two blokes followed them and that gives us a bit of breathing space. What we need to do now is leave and put as much distance as we can between us and them."

They left soon after. Bomber looked back as they climbed a hill behind the mysterious manor. He wanted to fix it in his memory, although he had a suspicion he would never be able to find it again.

They made good time and by mid-afternoon had left the deep wooded coombes and hills and were in more open countryside, wider fields and longer vistas across rolling hills and farm land. Jonno had studied Tom-Tom's maps minutely and had decided at any rate for now, for Sherborne for two reasons; one, it was in the right direction and two, Tom-Tom had made it look very attractive with two castles, one intact, one in ruins.

Chapter 4. A Night in the Library

They came to a crossroads of narrow lanes where Sherborne was signposted. Jonno decided they should go there and see if it was as good as Tom-Tom's map suggested. They walked for about an hour before reaching the outskirts. They passed near the Old Castle but realised it would be expensive to visit so went on to the town. They could see why Tom-Tom admired it. By chance they had arrived on Carnival Day. The High Street was crowded with visitors, bright stalls covered with striped awnings and many side-shows. Jonno and Bomber felt unaccountably relaxed and safe, protected by the good natured crowds who were happily eating hot dogs and ice cream and trying their skill or luck on various attractions. Both boys bought candy floss, the airy web of sugar fizzing on their tongues, reminding them of South London street fairs. Jonno won a coconut and Bomber succeeded in shooting five plastic ducks, thus securing a brown teddy bear which he quickly gave to a nearby small girl who was sobbing after failing to win one. Her mother thanked him gratefully and the father shook his hand.

They drank lemonade from a stall and as the crowd began to thin out at around 6 o'clock Jonno had an idea.

"We'll go to the library – we passed it on the way. It's an old building, looks as if it's got loads of little rooms. It closes at seven. I reckon if we go in there now we'll be able to hide there for the night. What do you say?"

"Sounds O.K. if we can get away with it."

They went back to the library and went in. It was, as Jonno had foretold, a warren of cosy little nooks and crannies, and, fortunately for the boys, still busy with last minute visitors. The librarians, two of them, had obviously put on an event as part of the carnival. They were occupied in looking at drawings and little stones which were part of some sort of competition for small children. The last of them finally made their way out by which time Jonno and Bomber had taken the opportunity to slip upstairs, find a book cupboard full

55

of dusty tomes and hide inside in the stifling darkness.

"I hope they don't lock this cupboard," whispered Bomber, trying not to sneeze.

"Why would they?" reasoned Jonno, "The whole place is full of books, more valuable than these."

"True, but I wish they'd hurry up and go home."

After about half an hour, Jonno could hear nothing, no voices or footsteps, so he cautiously looked out. All clear. He signalled to Bomber and they both crept to the head of the stairs leading from the upper gallery to the ground floor. Silence, except for distant sounds from the street outside. Jonno went quietly down to the main door. Locked.

"We've done it," he said to Bomber who was behind him, "We've got somewhere to stay for the night. Let's find the kitchen – there's got to be somewhere they make tea and stuff."

Before Bomber could answer, both he and Jonno were thrown heavily to the floor and, winded, were staring at two boys kneeling on their chests, one holding a knife, the other a heavy wooden plank of wood.

"What the hell are you two doing here?" demanded the one kneeling on Jonno. He looked about sixteen and his clothes were scruffy and dusty. Bomber's captor was similar in age and clothing but had fiery red hair. Jonno thought honesty was the best policy in the circumstances. The two looked threatening and ready to use their weapons at the slightest opportunity.

"We've escaped from the boys' home we were in and we're trying to get to Sussex without being caught by the people at the home or the police. This seemed a good place to stay for the night."

The two other boys seemed to accept this and, putting their weapons to one side, allowed Bomber and Jonno to stand up.

"O.K. You can stay for the night, one night only." Said the boy with red hair, as if he were inviting two guests into his home for the night. "We don't want to stay any longer. Anyway, what are you doing here?"

"It's one of our places we stay in round here. Sometimes we sleep in a barn about a mile away and there's an empty house, been empty for months, we sometimes go there."

"Have you run away from home, too?"

Red Hair looked pityingly at Jonno.

"We're not little kids, you weirdo," he said witheringly. "We don't have homes – we both left them ages ago. We're better off as we are, anyway."

"How come you haven't been caught by social services or the police? You must stand out like a sore thumb in a posh place like this; you can smell money a mile off and I bet most of the houses cost a million quid."

"Right," agreed Red Hair, "which makes it easier for us. No one expects us to be homeless. The few people, who do notice us, assume we're 'difficult', like skiving off school all the time. Anyway, we're not idiots. As I said we move around the area all the time."

"How do you manager for food?" asked Bomber who knew exactly how to obtain food in a large town but could not imagine how they would do it in a genteel town like Sherborne.

"Piss easy", he scoffed. "We visit Waitrose bins just after closing time. You must have done it."

"Yeah, we did, but that was in the middle of London and we had to fight loads of tramps. It was everyman for himself."

"You'd be surprised how many fight for the best stuff here. Most of them are just trying to save as much as they can on the housekeeping bills, but we manage pretty well, don't we Nick?"

The two boys had clearly accepted Jonno and Bomber into their property and showed them the office used by the librarians for a tea room. Apparently they knew about the boys and, provided they left no evidence, did not mind them using the tea, coffee, milk and sugar in the cupboard and fridge and apparently often left food for them overnight. That day, luckily, they had left tinned soup and a loaf so the four dined royally. Afterwards Jonno suggested a modified version of the Sine and Cosine game. Bomber marked out a board with some interesting hazards and nasty aliens. Red Hair (real name Dave) and Nick were intrigued by the game, so Dave and Jonno were Consines and the other two were Sines. The baddies and goodies soon became confused and in the end it was a riotous free for all.

"Why did you leave your Home," asked Nick. "It sounds pretty good to me, good food, nice and warm and the Uncles sound O.K. They didn't beat you up or anything, did they? I'd have stayed."

"All that is true," admitted Jonno, "But there was something a bit strange about them, though, which sort of made me wonder what they were up to."

"How do you mean?" Nick was intrigued, scenting a mystery.

"Well, they were kind to us in a distant sort of way, but they didn't have any sort of home life, private life, if you know what I mean. They weren't friends with the other Uncles. They would go away sometimes, but we never knew where, and, another thing, they never got angry or lost their temper with any of us."

Nick was silent for a moment then said, "Your Uncles sound robotic, or like aliens. No, I mean it," he said as Red Hair laughed derisively, "Their behaviour is just like aliens who are clever in most ways and can copy humans, except, they have no feelings."

"You could be right," said Jonno thoughtfully.

"I remember once when I first arrived there and Bomber didn't come till 3 days later and I was so fed up and miserable. I missed London, the noise, all the other boys in our gang. We looked out for each other and suddenly I was in this weird place. The Uncle who took me there seemed O.K. friendly and normal, but as soon as we arrived at the Home, he was, like, you know, cold. They are all like that; they help us, teach us properly. They seem to know everything, but now I come to think about it and now I'm away from them, they don't seem real."

"The thing that puzzles me about them most," said Bomber, "is what they get out of it?"

"How do you mean?" said Nick for the second time.

"Well, what I mean is, they must have a secret plan they're hatching, a hidden agenda. After all, it must cost shed loads of money to keep us. The Home is pretty luxurious, the food, although it's not my choice most of the time, is expensive stuff – you can tell. All the meat comes from an organic farm near the Home, the fruit and veg are all organic and –"

"Yes," interrupted Jonno, "And they send us to another Home to do 'A' levels, then they pay for us to go through Uni. I've looked the whole set up on the internet and there's not much to find, except, and this is really weird, it's described as a Home for disadvantaged boys – and the second Home is the same but, and this is even weirder, it says that they are both privately owned and funded."

"Is there anything else odd about them?" asked Red Hair.

"Well, they haven't got three eyes or anything like that," said Jonno, "but there is something strange, now I think about it."

The others, including Bomber, looked interested. Jonno continued, "Although the Uncles seem distant and like robots in a way in the day, at night when I had dreams, they were often in the dreams and they seemed normal and friendly and even had a laugh sometimes. The dreams were so real to me it was like they were really happening. It was mainly Uncle Jim and he used to help me revise and he told me once that the important thing I would be able to do was change people's minds, persuade them to do certain things. When I asked him how, he said 'with the power or words'".

Bomber said nothing. He thought how many times recently he had seen or rather, experienced, things which no one else had. Sometimes, he also had vivid dreams where he found himself in places he seemed to recognise, but not quite and often in a time that was not the present. He was certain the Uncles were aware of this. Once, after a particularly frightening dream, when he was in a W.W.I battle zone and he still felt uneasy the next day, Uncle Jim had said,

"Don't worry, David. You will be safe."

"What are you going to do tomorrow?" asked Nick.

"Just move on," answered Jonno vaguely, "see what's about."

"Why don't you hang around here for a bit?" suggested Red Hair.

"Tempting, but we've got to keep moving. I'm pretty certain we're being followed by someone or something. Our only chance is to keep one step ahead."

They talked for some time, cleared away after their meal then all four slept comfortably on the chairs and settee in the staff rest room. Up early they all prepared to leave by a side door leading to a deserted alleyway. Jonno and Bomber went towards the hill near the railway station which led to the main road out of the town. With mutual regret, they said goodbye to Nick and Red Hair, who went back toward the town.

Chapter 5. Cry Havoc

They strode forward briskly, reached villages like Thornford then Yetminster, all lazily murmuring in the warm day, with attractive stone cottages, pretty churches, tea rooms and village stores which sold everything. Both Bomber and Jonno, London born and bred, found these villages beguiling. They found little footpaths by streams, shallow and fast flowing, where silvery fish flashed by. They followed one meandering footpath for a while, then sat for a while by the side of the stream dangling their feet in the water and giggling as fishes tickled their toes.

"I wonder what it's like living in a place like this all the time," mused Bomber.

"O.K. for a while, I suppose, but what would we do? After a while we'd want to be off somewhere else. Anyway, these days, I bet nearly everyone who lives here commutes to the nearest big town. Apart from farming, what else is there to do?"

"I dunno. I've just thought – d'you remember that series we sometimes watched on the video? Uncle Jim used to watch them. 'Midsomer Murders', was it. Villages just like this, very pretty with roses round the door, thatched cottages, village greens, everyone speaking in posh voices, playing cricket for the blokes, the wives making jam for the village fete. In no time at all, someone would find a body, then there'd be another until the corpses were piling up and just one inspector and his sidekick would saunter in as if it was just an ordinary thing to happen like someone nicking a bar of chocolate from the village shop. Perhaps it's like that in these places. As we speak, an old lady is hideously stabbing her gardener to death, because he accidentally broke one of her roses."

Bomber suddenly stopped, his light hearted mood changing.

"Perhaps it's time to move on. We don't want to hang about too long or people will start noticing us and ask questions."

"You're worrying too much," replied Jonno, "In a place like this in the summer there are loads of visitors. But I see your point.

Time to leave. Come on."

They were soon out of the town and Jonno thought "It's almost like a normal time. We're on holiday, camping, exploring places like we would be doing if we had normal families, mum and dad, annoying sisters, cats…" He imagined himself and Bomber finding new places, fish and chips, setting up camp, being carefree.

Bomber broke in on his daydreams. "You know, Jonno, we need transport. We're not making enough headway."

So they walked more purposefully, going eastward, ignoring seductive signposts down narrow roads which sounded interesting. After a couple of hours of determined walking along a quiet road, a rare car passed them. It went by very slowly, then quickened and disappeared round the bend ahead. Jonno said, worried, "I don't like the look of that car. Did you see it was all black, blacked out windows, a sort of jeep?"

"You're right and look! It's stopped. I can just see the roof through the gap in that hedge."

"I don't want to risk going by it," Jonno declared, "Let's go through these trees where they won't know which way we've gone."

They moved fast through the thick overgrown patch of woodland, pushing through shrubs, brambles, muddy patches until they came to a clearing and a little farther on, a fairly steep abandoned quarry. Strangely, although the sides and broad base were thickly covered by long grass, tall wild flowers and many bushes, on the far side opposite to where the boys stood, a smooth, carefully cut, wide track led down to the quarry floor.

"Let's hide in the bushes down there until we're sure we weren't followed," suggested Bomber.

Their descent was easy and once on the quarry floor, they searched for a good hiding place. On pulling aside a particularly dense group of shrubbery, Jonno called urgently to Bomber who was exploring a few yards away.

"Look, here's an entrance to a cave or tunnel or something," he said with excitement. It was a miracle he'd found it. The wooden boarding that covered the entrance was entirely hidden by greenery and where Jonno had torn it away a small opening appeared where the wood had rotted.

"Brilliant," said Bomber, "let's hide in here till we know they've gone – that's assuming there were people in that car looking for us."

Jonno was happy to venture in, more because he loved the prospect of exploring rather than from fear of pursuit. They both had torches with them as essentials in their backpacks. They moved carefully into the blackness. Jonno switched on his torch. They appeared to be in a large cave with a dry earthen floor and smooth walls.

"This is man-made, not a natural cave," he said.

"You're not kidding – I can see that and I can see something else, too," answered Bomber.

"What?"

"This is still being used. Look the floor is trodden down hard and-" he stopped, then said, "there's a tunnel here, leading down there".

"Shall we go down it?" suggested Jonno.

It was too much to resist. They went in. the tunnel was narrow; they had to move singly and with caution – the floor was uneven.

"This gets more and more like Indiana Jones," said Bomber, "Anytime now we shall see a pit of copperhead snakes or the floor will open up and we'll be sealed in with a million rats, or –"

"Or we'll find a cave with a golden statue holding a priceless diamond worth a fortune," added Jonno.

Their carefree mood ended abruptly as they both heard something at the same time. Ahead of them, coming from some distance, was a muffled sound, difficult to define and intermittent. To the boys, it seemed like booming explosions mixed in with the sound of a chainsaw.

"What do you think it is?" mused Bomber, puzzled.

"Some sort of mining, I reckon," said Jonno, "though I can't imagine what's being mined down here."

Bomber suddenly knew that what was happening down there was dangerous and bad, ultimately evil. He could see, or partly see, a galleried cavern, full of cages containing things his mind didn't want to know about and beings in what looked like space suits.

"Come on, let's see what's going on," urged Jonno, "Indiana Jones would definitely carry on."

Bomber was reluctant but couldn't let Jonno go on alone so they moved on. The noise grew louder and a faint red glow suffused the tunnel making their torches unnecessary. They switched them off and went forward. The glow reddened and deepened, the explosions were more defined and the chainsaw noise was deafening. Silence. All noises ceased. After a few moments, the boys could faintly hear a murmur subdued. The boys hesitated then moved forward, more alert. The tunnel widened, the red glow became white like electric light. Without warning they were at the entrance to a cavern. Bomber's first thought; "this is hell. Somehow we've reached the Underworld." Then his second thought, "No, it can't be that. This is not one of my funny turns, this is real." Then he saw clearly what was in the Underground cavern. His earlier vision was partly explained. The cavern was a hive of activity, controlled and with purpose. The vast hall lit from an unseen source was indeed galleried. The uppermost tier, as far as the boys could tell was like an endless control panel with switches, lights flashing, figures in white suits sitting motionless in front of the panels. On the second gallery there were vats with huge rubbery hoses going in them and emitting an irregular liquid noise, like someone gulping. What was truly the stuff of nightmare was what was on the floor of the cave. Cages were placed at regular intervals, each one about six feet high and a foot square. Inside each one was a statue which, on more careful inspection, they saw was a person, with wires connected to their head and arms. Their bodies jerked and their heads slumped forwards. Some seemed old, many very much younger, male and female (although it was difficult to distinguish this, apart from the length of their hair). Further beings in while suit and helmets moved from cage to cage in a regular pattern, gazing at the cages then working on what appeared to be a tablet which they all carried. Bomber knew that they would both be in mortal danger if they were seen. He nudged Jonno and signalled his intention to turn round and retreat. Jonno was only too ready to comply. As he turned he noticed several metal containers nearby, all with 'W.D' painted in black on their sides. The boys moved fast and noiselessly down the tunnel. No longer fired with visions of Indiana Jones, the dread of being trapped in the nameless horror of the cavern made them able to run as they'd never run before, even when they'd run like a grey hound in the final relay in Sports Day against St. Andrews.

There was no sound of pursuit. After a while they slowed slightly. Jonno suddenly tripped on a piece of rope stretched across the floor. At once, pandemonium, an alarm signal shrieked from the direction of the cavern. The light was immediately extinguished, a drumming, faint at first but growing louder, louder, followed. "The hounds of hell are unleashed," thought Bomber, not knowing where the words had come from. They had a good start on their hunters and using their torches saw some landmarks, one being a rather repulsive large patch of, presumably, whitish mould, glinting paley by torchlight. They now knew they were near the entrance and in no time were outside. They raced across the quarry floor to the path they'd seen on their descent. They moved more quickly on the carefully cleared track and reached the top. The sound of shouts and answering calls gave them no time to take breath.

They were standing in the stubble of a cornfield, recently harvested. The sound of a tractor fairly close by comforted them. A tractor and his driver struck them as normal and every day and anyway thought Jonno, "we need to tell someone what we've seen." They went in the direction of the tractor and, climbing over a stile, found the tractor and the driver, a man about fifty, lean and brown, leaning against the trailer drinking from a large mug. A thermos flask was on the ground next to him. He seemed surprised to see them, amazed even, as he looked at them open mouthed.

"Where did you come from?" His tone implied they had been spirited there by a magician.

"From the quarry. Can you help us, please?" said Jonno breathlessly. Between them, they told him everything since their arrival at the quarry, their presence there explained by saying they were on a hiking/camping summer holiday.

The tractor driver listened.

"I know it sounds crazy," said Jonno, "but please believe us and please help us, because they are really after us. They know we saw them and what they were doing."

"I do believe you," replied the man. "I wouldn't if I lived anywhere else but here." This enigmatic statement momentarily puzzled Jonno. He had no time to ponder its significance as the sound of the hunters was in the distance, like hounds scenting their quarry.

"Quick," he said, "There's a gap under the tractor seat, not big and it'll be stuffy. Get in there and keep quiet." He lifted the seat and they squeezed into the confined space. They fitted themselves in and could breathe with reasonable ease through small gaps. Jonno briefly wondered why the driver hadn't told them to hide in the straw or hay (whatever it was) on the trailer. There was plenty of depth to cover them. The hunters were close and could be heard calling to one another. Soon they were outside. Barked commands, a short silence, then the tractor driver's voice, "Yes, I couldn't believe my eyes. Two lads, about fifteen I guess, like you said. They asked me where the nearest town was. I told them it was a fair distance in that direction. There aren't many cars round here, ever, of course. But they got lucky. On that track over there, a 4 X 4 turned up, stopped for them and off they went."

Sounds dying away; after a while – "O.K. You can come out now." They emerged into fresh air.

"Thanks so much for helping us," said Bomber.

"You're not out of the woods yet. They'll be back here soon enough. Look, I've got to take this load to a farm about twelve miles away out of the Controlled Area. It's in the opposite direction I sent them. I can take you to the farm then you'll have to make your own way."

Jonno and Bomber, relieved, climbed in beside the driver. He told them they would be safe for about five miles, then would have to hide under the seat as before as they would be on a road used by the hunters. As they set out, Bomber queried, "Why were you so surprised to see us and what did you mean when you said that this is a Controlled Area?"

"For a start you are in a very dangerous place here. All around here for miles belongs to the War Department. That means it's all highly secret, controlled by shady government people. Entry to anywhere in the zone is severely restricted. There are barriers on all the roads near here and big notices everywhere saying 'DANGER OF DEATH. KEEEP OUT'. How the hell did you manage to get in?"

"Well, for a start, I don't think they know about the way in at the bottom of the quarry or if they do, they think it's completely hidden and blocked off. By the way, why are you allowed in?"

"They allow a few of us on to the land to cultivate some of the fields but we are told nothing about what they are doing. We have never heard of an underground cavern or what's happening there. All that we know about is that from time to time we are completely denied access to the fields even if it's harvest time."

"What do they do?" asked Bomber.

"Good question. All I can tell you is that there are loads of explosions and at night the sky is lit up, blinding flashes of light, like a firework show."

The boys were quiet and Bomber remembered the metal cases marked 'W D'. "Must be some new weapons they're testing," He thought of the cages and their contents. Shuddering, he asked.

"What do you think they are doing down there in the quarry?"

"No idea and I don't want to know. It's very dangerous to get involved with anything going on with them." He made the word 'them' sound as if it was written in capital letters.

"I reckon they're testing on humans down there," said Jonno. "They must be using electricity or something".

"Whatever it is, they don't want anyone to know about it and –"

"Get under the seat, quick," said the tractor driver. His voice was urgent. The tractor stopped, he stood up, opened the seat, pushed the boys inside. The tractor started up again. Jonno and Bomber had an uncomfortable ride, being thrown about as well as being partly suffocated. The journey continued. The tractor came to a sudden halt. Voices, several voices. After about ten minutes the tractor restarted. Jonno estimated they'd been travelling for forty minutes. They stopped again. This time, the driver lifted the flap, saying, "This is it boys. Journey's end. No one about so scarper quickly."

"What happened earlier?" asked Bomber.

"You mean when I stopped? Two blokes stopped me and said they were searching for two boys who'd run away from home. Funny thing is – they didn't look like W.D. people. You two seem to be very popular. Everyone is after you. What have you done?"

"Actually, nothing," said Jonno. "We really haven't. Except run off," he added truthfully. "What did the two blokes look like?"

"Ordinary. Middle aged. One was nearly bald. Both wearing suits." Jonno looked at Bomber. One of the men following them at the garden party had been bald. They both guessed they were the same two. They thanked the tractor driver who wished them luck and continued on his way. The boys looked around. They were at the start of a long, very wide street. Tree lined, with elegant buildings and shops it stretched straight ahead, inviting. Jonno and Bomber saw several people leaning over a railing on one side, looking down. They went over and saw a clear, quite deep and fast flowing river. Looking closer they were aware of large silvery fish flashing by.

A small girl threw bread into the water; a ripple, a mouth opened, the bread was gone. Mesmerised by the movement, Jonno and Bomber stood side by side. Jonno became aware that a man was standing very close beside him, pressing against him. He tried to move towards Bomber but Bomber was pushing against him. "Don't try to get away. We're going to walk quietly away to the car." The boys were both held in a vice like grip and propelled to a nearby car, pushed in as the car moved forward.

"Where are you taking us?" asked Jonno. Their abduction had been so swift; he'd not even had time to look at the men. He was in the back with one of his captors, Bomber in the front by the driver. He could see at once they were not the two who had pursued them to the party. Bomber thought, "These are from the quarry. They are taking us underground to torture us. No one will ever know." Deep depression then – realisation that he could try to save them both. Some time ago it had dawned on him that he and several of the Uncles were telepathic. Also it worked the other way. Just as he could, with concentration, cloak his thoughts so that they could not find him, so he could send them messages by fixing his mind on what he wanted the Uncles to know.

Worth a try. As the car sped on, Bomber visualised the landscape, the stern warning notices, the quarry, the tunnel, the cavern, the cages. He appealed to the Uncles. Save us, please.

And they answered. A few miles on, in the middle of nowhere with 'DANGER OF DEATH – KEEP OUT' just ahead, the car stopped abruptly. A barrier barred them. Two figures in army uniform approached with rifles. Their two captors looked puzzled.

"What's this then?" asked the driver.

"Orders," His reply was terse. "Get out, you two and in there." He indicated a jeep nearby with 'WD' on the side. "You two carry on" to the driver.

They hurried Jonno and Bomber over to the waiting car and drove off at top speed.

"It won't be long before they're after us," said the driver taking off his army helmet. The boys recognised the bald man.

"Where are you taking us?" asked Jonno.

"Where do you want to go?" An unexpected response.

"Midhurst," replied Bomber. The response had entered his mind, clearly defined. He did not know why.

"Midhurst it shall be," the bald man answered.

They drove for some time. The two men were silent yet strangely, given the circumstances, their silence, to Bomber, seemed companiable rather than hostile. Jonno was thinking, deeply about their situation. These men. Who were they? Friend or foe? They had clearly been chasing them from the time the two of them had left the Home, yet now they appeared to be friends rather than foes. Jonno, nevertheless, was uneasy. What was their plan? And, biggest question of all – how had they known about the boys' great danger at the hands of the sinister WD?

Bomber's thoughts on the car journey were rather different. He knew very well why they had been saved just in time from a fate he didn't want to think about. He had sent a clear and urgent message to the Uncles and they, or rather, their henchmen, had responded immediately. Bomber had sent them an accurate visual representation of the quarry, the tunnel, its unspeakable contents and a clear indication of the countryside around. The overwhelming question in his mind was how he should use this power he had been given. It should not be used lightly, he knew. If he did, he also knew, it would be withdrawn, permanently. With regard to the two henchmen, he instinctively understood they were really neither friend nor foe. They were at the beck and call of the Uncles, would not know their whereabouts unless he, Bomber, told them in his thoughts. Every day he was learning better how to cloak his thoughts.

They drove for a long time, through Wiltshire, through the wide

fields of Hampshire. Jonno recognised sign posts and road numbers
from Tom-Tom's maps. He saw with delight they were on Tom-
Tom's favourite road, the A272. He had devoted the whole of
one map entirely to this meandering road which began (or ended,
according to your point of view) around Maresfield in East Sussex
and ends at Stockbridge a long way away on the edge of Hampshire
where it meets Wiltshire. They went through Bramdean, which, on
Tom-Tom's chart, highlighted the Watercress Line, not far to the
north. There was an engaging picture of a steam engine, snorting
plumes of steam and a little further, a banger racing circuit. Jonno
thought longingly of both and resolved to visit both if ever they
were free and able to live like everyone else. Petersfield was next and
a signpost which read 'Butser Ancient Archaeological Farm'. Jonno
knew about this place. On a fairly remote location near Petersfield,
an ancient farm and village had been re-created, surrounded by Iron
Age crops such as spelt and emmer. A few of the boys at the Home
who were particularly absorbed by ancient history, had spent what
sounded like a fantastic weekend there a few months ago. Jonno
had listened to their account of this with great regret that he had
not gone with them. There was a massive Iron Age roundhouse,
the lucky boys had told him, where they slept – on animal skins –
and cooked vegetables over an open fire in the middle of the vast
earthen floor. The man and woman in charge wore long tunics
and said they were druids. It happened to be full moon and the
druids told them that such a time was vitally important. The
boys, apparently, found the midnight ceremony in the light of the
full moon 'freaky'. They enjoyed the following day, though. In a
faithfully recreated Roman villa they had a Roman banquet, made up
of roast rabbit, pigeon, duck and lamb and – beef burgers.
"Beef burger?" Jonno remembered querying.
"Yes," one of the boys had replied. "The druids told us that the
Romans loved eating burgers."
The high spot for all those who hadn't gone on the trip was the

present the boys brought back for them. They gave everyone, even the Uncles, a bag of sheep droppings. They certainly looked like sheep poo, but, mysteriously, tasted like peppermint.

Chapter 6. A Game of Chess

"Midhurst, as requested". Jonno and Bomber were startled. Both had
been deep in thought, lulled by the long car journey.

"Thanks very much," Bomber climbed out stiffly, followed by
Bomber.

"Hope you're both good at chess," remarked one of the drivers as
they drove off.

"Why the hell did he say that?", said Jonno.

"Haven't a clue," replied Bomber, a touch apprehensive, since the
two men were usually uncommunicative, speaking only when
absolutely necessary.

Decision time. In front of them, a raised wide grassy track led to a
ruined building, difficult to tell what it had once been. On their left a
large sign, 'Polo today'. Sounds of cheering and general hubbub.

"Polo?", queried Bomber, thinking of peppermints.

"It's a posh people's game. You ride a pony chasing a ball or
something round the pitch, using a sort of stick."

"Like hockey on horseback?" suggested Bomber.

"Let's take a look."

They followed the noise and reached a large crowd surrounding the
game, which they could barely see. Next to the crowd, on another
part of the field, several boys and some girls were standing around,
some in pairs, some singly. "They look a bit weird," thought Jonno,
"what are they up to?"

"Those kids look strange, you're right", said Bomber, reading his
thoughts.

They went nearer. Two boys, near them, were standing motionless,
talking to each other in subdued voices, meanwhile fixedly staring
ahead. A girl, alone, stood a little way off, also staring in the same
direction. Jonno couldn't understand what they were doing. Bomber
said, "I know what this is, a chess game. They're playing chess. Look,
the field is marked in squares."

And so it was. Small stones outlined the squares.

The boys were playing the girls. There were more girls on the grass chess board than boys. The girls were clearly in the ascendant, the boys struggling. Both Jonno and Bomber were accomplished players, since Uncle Jim had insisted all the boys learn chess.

"Chess is the best way to learn how to outwit your friends and outmanoeuvre your enemies. Learn to look ahead, work out their next moves and be one step ahead."

"That boy over there, the bishop, will be in trouble unless he moves quickly." (All the boys wore black tops, the girls white tops, with the part they were playing inscribed on their backs) Jonno moved over to him, stood near him and whispered advice. The bishop, beckoned to him. "Come and work with me," he said. "I could do with some help."

Bomber, intrigued, approached. Another boy, a Knight, called to him, "Why don't you help me?"

Both Bomber and Jonno soon discovered that the boys were outplayed by the girls, so were happy to join the game. No one seemed to mind and the girls clearly felt that two more boys were no threat. Finally, in spite of Jonno's and Bomber's input, sometime later, the girls triumphantly called "checkmate" and everyone cheered, even the boys. They all left the green chess board and gathered in groups under some trees.

"Thanks for helping," said one boy to Jonno and Bomber, "You stopped us losing quite so badly. The girls always humiliate us every year. This time we lasted longer."

"Come and have some food with us, if you're not in a hurry. The winners have to buy food for the losers so it's not all bad," added the boy helped by Bomber.

Neither the boys nor the girls showed any curiosity about Jonno and Bomber as they all invaded the not-too-distant Macdonald's. Afterwards they all returned to the polo/chess field. The polo match was over, the crowd had dispersed and in another part of the estate, there was great activity. A stage was in the process of erection with all the attendant electricians, stagehands, construction builders and noise.

"It looks like Glastonbury," said Bomber. "What's going on?"

"It's going to be fantastic, brilliant," enthused Ben, Jonno's chess companion. "We've had an incredible stroke of luck. Alt-J are doing a gig for us here tonight."

"How the hell did you manage that?" asked Bomber "They only play places like Manchester, Brighton or the O2.

"True, but one of our mate's brother was at uni with Gus, the lead singer and he asked him if he'd play here for charity."

"So they're actually coming here?"

"They certainly are, in the flesh. Do you want to stay and see them?"

"Would we? That's a no-brainer," replied Bomber, who still couldn't really believe it. Alt-J was one of his favourite bands. Since he had first heard them way back before their rise to universal acclaim, he had loved their innovative style of indie rock, but had never actually been to any of their concerts. He and Jonno temporarily forgot their plans, the possibility of pursuit and, with the rest, waited impatiently for the evening event.

At last, at around 8.30 with long shadows in the late sunshine, the band came on stage and Gus sang with Thom and Joe accompanying him. The crowd loved it all, clapping, cheering, yelling for more after each turn. Bomber was beside himself with excitement, nearly hoarse with shouting encouragement and approval. When the band finished their final song, after uncounted encores, Bomber found himself, with Jonno and several others, backstage in the mothy moonlight drinking black coffee with Alt J. They sat on the boards and the grass. Gus, Thom and Joe, winding down after a long evening, lounged against part of the stage with a very tall fair haired boy about the same age as Gus, or perhaps a few years younger. His name was Troy and he was a cousin of Gus. Jonno sat by him and they were immediately friends.

"Do you live here?" asked Troy.

"No, I don't really live anywhere," replied Jonno.

"Explain", demanded Troy.

"Well, we're on the run, actually." This from Jonno who instinctively felt he could trust Troy with anything.

"Sounds interesting, tell me more."

Between them, Jonno and Bomber told him their story, finishing with their problem with the Uncles – were they trying to recapture the boys?

"Are you sure the two men who followed you are connected with the Uncles?" asked Troy.

"Who else could they be working for?" answered Bomber.

"Look at it from a different angle," replied Troy "Other people or organisations, apart from the Uncles might be interested in you. They could be very interested in fact."

"Such as?" queried Jonno.

"For a start, certain political parties would be very glad to use the ability you tell us you have, Bomber, of visualising things from the past, present and future. They could make accurate predictions of future events. Just think of the power that would give them. You must see my point."

"I guess so, and they would find Jonno even more useful with the way he can persuade people to believe everything he says – He can even make me believe him sometimes." said Bomber, laughing.

"So you reckon our hunters are keeping an eye on us, to see what we're up to, where we're going?"

"Well, they could be, or, on the other hand they could be working for the Uncles, just letting you have a taste of freedom, but watching you and keeping you out of danger."

"And then reeling us in like fish at the end of the line when they want us back," added Jonno.

"Anything's possible, but it's all a bit weird I must admit," said Troy.

"Are they around now, I wonder, lurking behind bushes or sneaking up behind us." He said this jokingly.

Nevertheless Jonno and Bomber looked nervously around, beyond the range of the glare cast by the stage lights. Later, after more coffee and burgers with Alt-J and several boys and girls, they accepted the offer of sharing a tent with two of the boys. The field had become a mini Glastonbury for the night with many tents and a larger one with primitive washing facilities and a composted toilet. Alt-J departed in their rather sumptuous converted bus at around midnight for their next gig, taking Troy with them as far as Brighton, as he had to return for lectures at his uni there, the following morning.

"Shame I've got to go back," he said, "otherwise I'd love to come with you. Sounds like a great gag. Keep in touch. Let me know how it all falls out."

In the morning, after an interesting breakfast of cold burgers and chips with cocopops, they parted from their new friends and started to walk across country in more or less an easterly direction. There was a fine drizzle in the air and they found it hard to share Troy's assertion that it was all a 'great gag'. From time to time they glanced nervously about, remembering his other light hearted reference to men 'lurking behind bushes'. They covered quite a distance across heathland, woodland then followed a farm track which seemed to be heading in the right direction. They saw hardly anyone on their journey, a few dog walkers, three horses with their riders and, more worryingly, a man with a shot gun carrying a bulging bag, accompanied by a woman with a very hard face who stared at the boys fixedly. The man also looked closely at them; they then strolled off in the opposite direction.

"I didn't like the look of those two," remarked Bomber, watching them uneasily.

"No, very nasty. She looked like the first head we had at our infants' school. Wouldn't like to meet her on a dark night," replied Jonno.

"The bloke with the gun didn't look too friendly either. Hope they've gone for good."

They walked for another couple of miles past a large farmhouse and surrounding fields with cows and sheep as well as quite a few farm buildings, animal pens, barns and outbuildings. They went into the farthest barn, which was set up with a work bench, many assorted tools and stools, plus an ancient but comfortable sofa. The whole place smelt pleasantly of wood shavings and hay. There was clearly no one about so they risked resting on the sofa for a while as the drizzle was now definitely rain and they were tired.

"We're going to have to find some food soon, I'm starving," said Jonno.

"Me too and we'll have to find somewhere to sleep later. This rain's a bit of a downer," agreed Bomber.

They had passed a kitchen garden well stocked with carrots and a greenhouse with tomatoes and lettuces, all well out of sight of the farmhouse and, hopefully, watching eyes. However the prospect of a raw salad of stolen vegetable and scrumped unripe apples was not alluring. They stayed for an hour or so then decided to find a village where they might be able to do a few jobs for the local village shopkeeper, buy some food and even find an outhouse or barn for the night. The first part of the plan was accomplished and went well. They arrived at a pretty village with the required local shop/cum post office. The village square was bustling with young children playing on swings on the little green in the centre while their mothers chatted, older children gathered in small groups eating sweets and talking, older people relaxing on seats set around the square and the shop itself was clearly busy. To the two boys it seemed an idyllic country scene with no danger of sinister watchers anywhere near.

They entered the shop and waited their turn. A friendly looking woman behind the counter smiled at them. "Can I help you?" she asked.

Encouraged by her attitude, Jonno came straight to the point. "We're on a walking holiday and we've run out of money," he explained.

"We wondered if you've got any jobs you want done, like clearing up or delivering stuff around the village, please, then we can earn enough to buy some food from the shop."

At first she looked surprised, then, after a few moments said, "Well, I could do with a bit of help this afternoon. My usual young man rang in sick and I've got a lot of deliveries to people and I need to get tea for my three." Her three were three pleasant children, clustered in the inner doorway of the shop which clearly led to a living room. The oldest, a girl of about eight years, had quite long fair hair and a vivid, lively face. A boy, aged about six stood on one leg beside her holding a toy helicopter made of lego. He had brown curly hair and large brown eyes and, like his sister, looked full of mischief and life. The youngest, a little boy of about two years old, looked like a small copy of his sister and was grinning widely at Jonno and Bomber.

"Would you take these boxes of shopping to the people on the label. Oh damn! I forgot, there are no addresses because Chris knows where everyone lives."

"We can help, Mum. James and I know everyone in the village and where they live. We can show them. Please let us, Mum, please," said the young girl.

Her mother thought for a moment clearly summing the boys up, then "O.K, Cerys. That's a good idea and I can carry on here. Alright boys? Would you do that?" said Mrs Robinson, the shop keeper.

The boys were delighted and took the first box with Cerys and James in close attendance, giving a running commentary on where they were going and their assessment of the recipient of the goods. Their comments on each person in each house they subsequently visited were, to say the least, frank. As they went up to the front door of a rose covered cottage, Cerys announced loudly "Mrs Carlson's a witch. Everyone knows she is. She makes spells and Lloyd, my friend, said that once she turned a boy into a werewolf. Did you hear what I said Jonno? I said –"

"Yes, I heard what you said Cerys. Very interesting," replied Jonno hastily, as the "witch" opened the door. A pleasant faced, frail elderly lady asked the boys to put the box in the hallway, thanked them with a smile as she closed the door.

"See what we mean?" hissed Cerys as they went back to the shop for the next box.

"Oh, definitely," replied Bomber, "It's lucky for us she didn't magic us all into mice."

"You don't believe us," said Cerys accusingly.

"Oh we do, of course we do. We've known some fairly nasty people in our time, haven't we Jonno?"

"Tell us about them", said James eagerly.

"Well, a couple, a man and woman, passed us on our way here and we didn't like the look of them at all, did we, Jonno?"

"No, they looked very spooky and horrible."

"Tell us about them," said James, his brown eyes even bigger than ever with delight.

"They just had nasty faces, you know what I mean, thin faces, small mean looking eyes and very thin lips – oh, and the man had a gun." Cerys looked unimpressed. "That's nothing," she said, "He'd probably been out shooting clay pigeons. They do that all the time up at the farm.

Cerys and James enthusiastically accompanied the boys as they completed the delivery of the food boxes. Mrs Robinson, their mother was just closing the shop as they finished.

"Mum, can Jonno and Bomber stay for tea, please? Please, mum," asked Cerys.

"I've already laid a place for them," she answered, "It's shepherd's pie, then apple crumble. Is that O.K?"

"Yes, please, we're starving," answered Jonno.

After a delicious and sustaining meal, both Bomber and Jonno felt ready for anything and prepared to leave, Mrs Robinson gave them a generous wage in return for their help. In spite of their protests that it was too much, she insisted they should take it and packed sandwiches and cake for later.

They walked to the front door (which was on the side of the house and led to a path, leading to the back garden and the front of the shop). Cerys and James were ahead and suddenly,

"Stop!" commanded Cerys, peering through the small window at the side of the shop.

"What's up?" asked Jonno.

"You told us you'd seen two nasty people and the man had a gun."

"Yes, we did," agreed Jonno.

"Well, two people like that are standing on the other side of the square. Look," and she pointed out of the window.

"They are the same two," said Bomber, worried "We'll never get past them without being seen."

"I know," said Cerys, "We can help. Come round to the garden down the side path. You can hide in the garden shed until they've gone away."

"That's a really good idea, but they might hang around for ages," replied Jonno.

"No they won't," said James, "Not if we tell them you went on that bus that stopped outside the shop a little while ago."

And it worked. Cerys and James returned with the news that the couple had asked them as they came into the square to ride their bikes whether they had seen two boys. Apparently they described Jonno and Bomber accurately and told the two children that they were the boys' parents and they had come to pick them up as they'd rung them for a lift.

"We told them you'd got on the bus and they looked at each other, then they said "Thanks" and went to a car near them and drove off."

"They went very fast, about a 100 miles an hour," added James gleefully.

"Where was the bus going?" asked Bomber.

"To Renton," answered James. "We know that because our Nan lives there. It's a long way."

"You two have been brilliant. We couldn't have managed without you," said Jonno and Bomber nodded vigorously in agreement.

"It's been fun. Will you come back again?" asked Cerys.

"Definitely. We'll come back one day to see you and tell you what happened on our adventure."

They walked fast in the opposite direction to the bus route, striding across a nearby field to more wooded country where they were less likely to be seen. They considered their situation as they walked.

"It looks to me as if there are two different sets of people after us," said Jonno, thoughtfully. "I reckon the Uncles have sent people to sort of spy on us but they don't seem to be actually out to catch us."

"Yeah, it could be they are keeping an eye on us to make sure we're O.K. Those two that rescued us from the quarry and took us to Midhurst must be on our side, well sort of, anyway", replied Bomber. "What about the others?"

"Probably something to do with the other two we've just got away from They didn't seem as if they wanted to help us. They could be connected to the quarry people." This from Jonno.

"You could be right. I reckon they will be after us. For a start, they know we saw exactly what was going on there," Bomber shuddered and continued, "whatever it is, it's probably illegal and even the W.D, whoever they are, don't know about it. They'll want to trap us before we can report them to the police."

"What do you think they'll do to us?" pondered Jonno.

"Whatever it is, it won't be nice," answered Bomber.

They moved even faster, looking left and right and behind as they covered several miles of remote downland, hillsides full of wild flowers and gorse and strips of woodland. They avoided all tracks, paths and roads. Reaching a ridge, a steep grassy slope lay before them and at the bottom a single railway line.

"Where d'you think that goes to?" said Bomber.

"Dunno, but it's obviously not in use, so we might as well follow it for a while," proposed Jonno.

"O.K, I'm up for that. At least it's on the flat and a change from climbing all these hills. I'm not so sure it's unused. These rails are quite shiny and look, there are bits of coal along the track"

"You could be right, Bomber. All the same, let's walk along or by the side of it, when there's room."

They followed the line, sometimes it ran straight ahead and they could see the line narrowing to a point, then it would curve, to reveal a different vista. After a wide arc they came suddenly upon a little wooden hut right beside the line. "I've seen these sort of huts before," said Jonno. "They used to be for the men who worked on the track in the old days when there were steam engines.

"What's inside?" asked Bomber.

"Not sure, let's have a look," replied Jonno.

They approached with care, pushed the heavy wooden door and looked inside. It was very dark. After a while, as their eyes became accustomed to the gloom, they saw a fire place, laid with paper, wood and a bucket of coat next to it. There was a bench with a tin jug and two tin mugs and two very old and dirty armchairs with stuffing bulging out.

"Looks to me as if it's still being used," said Bomber. "There's a packet of sugar on the bench and this jug has got water in it."

"I know what this is," exclaimed Jonno. "This is a hut for people who work on the railway, now. It's still running, I bet. You know the sort of railway I mean, like the Watercress Line. People love them. They have steam engines and old fashioned coaches. Don't you remember that old film the Uncles showed us the first Christmas we were at the Home? I remember, it was called 'The Railway Children', all about some kids a long time ago who lived by a steam railway. It was a bit boring, but the Uncles loved it."

"Yes, now you mention it, I do remember and this must be one of them. Perhaps it is the Watercress Line. It must be round here somewhere."

"Why don't we stay here for the night? Even if this line is still in use there won't be any more trains this late and we can make tea and eat the stuff Mrs Robinson gave us. I'm knackered, anyway after all that walking."

"Yeah, it was a bit of a route march," said Bomber, "and I'm knackered, too. Those arm chairs don't look too clean but who cares?"

They were more exhausted than even they realised and after making some rather smoky black tea on the fire they had lit and eating the sandwiches and cake, they slept almost immediately. As Jonno slept he went to his Other Place almost straightaway. No Uncles, a children's playground he recognised. This was the polluted school yard with, at first glance, happy children running and skipping, but another look revealed the monstrous deformities, a little girl with chicken legs and claws, a boy's body with a dog's head. Jonno knew, now, the significance of his dream. With absolute certainty he understood that this dream, which he first encountered weeks before, told him precisely about the scene he and Bomber saw in the underground cavern. The dream was not a scene from Jonno's overactive imagination; which Tom-Tom often referred to, but a version of a rather nasty truth. He awoke suddenly, immediately wide awake. The man and woman were standing by the boys. Bomber was stirring.

"Get up," commanded the woman very coldly. Jonno, like a robot, heaved himself out of the ancient armchair and stood dully. Bomber did the same. Without speaking, their captors took them out of the hut and marched them swiftly up the grassy bank, the woman gripping Jonno's arm, the man taking Bomber's arm.

"Where are you taking us?" said Jonno. No reply. He briefly considered making a run for it, convinced that Bomber would do the same. "No, wouldn't work," he thought. "They've got transport ready nearby somewhere. I'm pretty certain they're not working for the Uncles. Those other two men who rescued us from the W.D. could be part of the Uncle set up." Suddenly he knew where these two captors came from. "Of course, they are from the W.D. They're taking us back there, to the quarry." Jonno was terrified, really terrified for the first time.

"Are you taking us back to the quarry?" he asked, hating the way his voice faltered, betraying his fear.

No answer. Bomber, meanwhile, was busy thinking very hard. He had arrived at the same answer as Jonno and was ready with a way out. When they had been in grave danger at the quarry at the hands of their pursuers, he, Bomber, had visualised their predicament, their location, their captors and in his mind, sent it to whoever was receptive. The first two men had arrived very quickly. Bomber did the same thing, he painted what he hoped would be an accurate picture of the railway track, the field they were crossing which was bordering a country road. A car was parked behind a hedge they were walking towards. Unfortunately, Jonno's voice broke his mental concentration "Are you going to kill us?" he asked his captor.

"Don't be ridiculous." Her voice was snappy.

"What then?" said Jonno "Are you taking us to the police?"

This time the man answered, "No, you've no need to worry. You're coming back with us for a short while, then you can carry on with whatever you're doing." His voice was like treacle Bomber thought and at once knew exactly what was in store for them both; a spell in the cavern with wires attached to their heads and bodies. Now he understood what was happening down there in the nightmare cave. The experiments were on mind control. People were being conditioned to behave, think in a certain way. In two books he'd read from the library at the Home, '1984' and 'Brave New World', the writers had drawn a grim picture of mind control experiments. Bomber thought, "I must act quickly." He saw they were rapidly approaching the car. He resumed his interrupted concentration on their dire situation. His message was urgent, "Come here, to this place, Now."

Chapter 7. The Noose Tightens

Breaking the early morning birdsong and trees whispering in the
light breeze, came the sound of voices, many voices, carefree and
laughing. A group of about fifteen schoolgirls, in white tops and
deep blue skirts with clipboards in their hands and accompanied by
four women, presumably teachers, were standing by the car, listening
to one of the teachers, but chatting amongst themselves, as well.
Bomber knew his call had been answered. The group saw Bomber,
Jonno and their captors approaching.

"Hi," called one of the girls, fair haired and quite tall. "Look what
we've found," and she pointed to the hedge.

"Excuse me, do you mind moving away from the car. We're in a
hurry," ordered the man, still firmly gripping Bomber's arm.

"Just come and see this first, it's an absolute miracle," said the same
girl. Bomber knew they were safe and he knew too, that this fair
haired girl, like him, could 'see' things, like him, sometimes, from the
past and future, as well as the present.

"What is it?" he said, entering into the game she was secretly playing
to ensure their escape.

"Look, it's the caterpillar of the Privet Hawk Moth," she said
breathless and excited.

"What's so special about it, Letty?"

"Dumbo! They're a really endangered species, almost extinct and
we've found one. After all, we are supposed to be studying the plant
and animal life of this area, so this is an absolute treasure trove – or
something like that," added Letty.

"They all crowded round the bush Letty was pointing at and stared
at the large green caterpillar with a fearsome black spike sticking up
from its final segment.

"That looks dangerous," remarked Bomber, who like Jonno had
broken away from their captors to join the girls round the privet
hedge.

"No, it's not," explained Letty, "It's protection for the caterpillar to stop birds eating it. They're really harmless and they turn into fantastic moths, about six inches across their wings. And this one proves they're alive and kicking down here."

"Excuse me, please," repeated the man, this time making a determined effort to propel Bomber into the car, the woman doing the same with Jonno. Once, the boys were safely in, the other two climbed in and waited for the girls to move aside as they were still clustered round the car, particularly Letty, who was leaning against the bonnet. Losing patience, the man attempted to start the car, which coughed once or twice then died. The man, red faced and angry continued to try to start the car. He finally got out, followed closely by Jonno and Bomber.

"Damn! We've got to get these boys to Woodbridge urgently. I can't believe this car. It's never let us down before."

"Don't worry," said one of the teachers, a plump and middle aged woman in jeans and a t-shirt with 'Merton Hill School' emblazoned across the back. "We'll get you there. I've just rung the coach driver who's with us for our field trip. He's parked in a lay by just round the corner. Ah! Here he comes. All aboard, everyone."

"Oh! Thanks," said Jonno, inventively. "These two people offered to drive us there to meet our parents. Now, if you're going that way, they don't have to worry about us. Thank you all the same. Hope you get the car started," he added, turning to the man and woman who stood speechless and red faced with anger.

The coach edged its way cautiously along the narrow road, meeting no traffic until they reached a wider route. Bomber sat by Letty.

"You heard me, didn't you," he said to her. It was more of a statement than a question.

"Of course I did," she answered. "I'm so glad to meet you at last. I've been listening to you for quite some time, you know."

"No I didn't know. I can send messages if I concentrate really hard and I do have visions, sort of. Sometimes I know what they mean but not who sends them."

"Do you remember, not long ago, standing in a stone circle and you felt the stone you were leaning against was alive, like a heart beating?" asked Letty.

"Yes, I did. How do you know?" asked Bomber.

"I was there, too. We were in old time just for a moment and I met you. Soon you will be able to meet people in places everywhere and in different times easily."

"What will we have to do?" asked Bomber.

"Could be anything, but there will be a purpose. We will have to intervene in a certain time in a certain place to do something to change the situation."

"It's such a relief to know someone else like me. Sometimes I see things which no one else does, of course, and they scare me."

"They scare me, too, but I always come back and you will too."

"Perhaps," said Bomber, "but I'm not too sure of that."

"I know one thing for sure," said Letty, "and that is, you and I will meet lots of times in lots of places."

"I'm glad about that," answered Bomber.

She smiled at him and briefly touched his hand.

He added. "Are all your friends here special? Where do you live?"

"We're sort of your sister school. We live in a Home for disadvantaged girls exactly like yours, except you're boys."

"And do you have Aunts in charge?"

"Of course, just like your Uncles."

"Do all of you have a special thing you're really good at, like us?"

"Yes, just like you. By the way, why did you and Jonno run away?"

"You guessed then?"

"Yes, and I could see those two people with you were dangerous. What had happened?"

Bomber told her the whole story of their planned escape and their subsequent adventures. He also confessed how he and Jonno had thought the Uncles had some sinister, hidden plans for the boys, though he admitted they seemed to be watching over them both since they obviously knew their whereabouts and had probably saved the two of them from the terrors of the quarry.

"I bet they even knew about your plans for leaving all the time," said Letty.

"Why didn't they stop us then?" asked Bomber.

"They probably wanted you to find out about everything for yourselves. After all, they needed you both to realise they weren't evil. Mind you, they're the other halves of the Aunts if you see what I mean, and I haven't completely sussed them out, either."

"In what way do you mean?", queried Bomber.

"It's like this, they are really helpful and like at your Home, they teach us brilliantly. We all do well in exams. We take most of our GCSEs early, well before we're sixteen. It's difficult to explain, but one of the things that makes them seem a bit weird is that they don't have a life outside the Home. They don't even socialise with each other. They never go on holiday and they don't appear to do anything except teach. You'd think the young ones would have boyfriends but we've never seen any."

"Once or twice," said Bomber, "I've had this creepy feeling that the Uncles are robots, almost, as if they are programmed to do certain things to make them look human."

"Or something worse," added Letty.

"Such as?" said Bomber.

"I know it sounds crazy," said Letty, "but they could even be aliens."

"You've been watching too much 'Dr Who'", Bomber laughed, uneasily.

"O.K. so I'm stupid, but listen to this. I can usually work out what people are thinking about if I concentrate my mind on them. I've always been able to do it, even when I was very young. And when I try to connect with any of the Aunts, there's nothing, nothing at all. It's as if they don't exist. It's creepy."

"That is creepy, but are you sure they're not hiding their thoughts deliberately? I can do that, and I can send thought messages to the

Uncles like I told you."

"You're probably right," said Letty, "Anyway I realised how different we are at the Home, from girls at normal schools, and living at normal family homes. We play lacrosse and netball with local schools and we chat to them and sometimes text them when the Aunts aren't looking. We can tell they can't do things we can and they don't do nearly as many GCSEs as us or know the stuff we know. We must seem like aliens to them, like they seem like dimbos to us."

At which point in the conversation, the coach stopped for the boys to leave, as the girls had reached their destination. As they left, Bomber said quietly to Letty, "See you again?"

She whispered back, "Of course you will. You know we'll meet up again."

"That's good," said Bomber. "By the way, how did you stop the car from starting? It must have been you."

She smiled and took an object out of her bag. "The rotor arm," she said.

Chapter 8. Peril in the Treetops

Jonno and Bomber stood in a quiet side street on the edge of a quite large town. The coach driver had pointed the way into town and had confirmed there was a railway station and bus station near the town centre. The two boys walked in this direction as they considered their next move. Chichester, therefore Runcton and Uncle Tom, were not too far away now. Jonno was excited. The thoughts of Runcton, the orchard, chickens, warn brown eggs and Uncle Tom's warmth made his heart thump in his chest. He and Bomber stopped at a small general store, just before the main shops in the High Street, bought pies, chocolate and cans of coke and sat on a seat by the War Memorial to eat their food. The sat quietly, each thinking deeply.

"Hi, chaps, how are things with you, today?" The voice startled them both. A man of about twenty five to thirty years old was sitting on the bench beside them. They had not heard or seen his approach. He was dressed in a smartly casual way with dark trousers and jacket and an open neck shirt. He carried a briefcase and, to the boys, looked confident and pleasant. As they considered their response, he spoke again.

"Am I right in thinking you are both from Oakhurst School?" he asked tentatively.

"How did you know? Are you psychic?" asked Jonno, amazed.

"In answer to your second question, yes I am. To answer your first question, because I can read and I can see the name written on your back pack. Small letters admittedly but just about legible."

"Yes, we are," replied Jonno, guardedly, "We're on a walking holiday and we're on our way back soon – and we don't need a lift, thanks all the same." He added this quickly.

"I wasn't going to offer you a lift." The young man sounded amused. "What I will offer you instead, is tea, coffee of coke over there in Caffe Nero."

The three of them were soon sitting very comfortably at a round table in the bay window on arm chairs, the boys drinking hot chocolate. Their companion, Ben, as he'd introduced himself, chose a pot of Earl Grey tea.

"I'll come clean straightaway," said Ben. "I know all about your Home and when I saw the name on your rucksack, I had to talk to you. You see, I went there, too."

Jonno and Bomber were astonished and for a few moments, speechless. Then, "Did you like it?" asked Jonno eagerly.

"Did you have the same Uncles, Uncle Jim, Uncle Bob?" This from Bomber.

"Yes to both questions," said Ben, "but now answer my question, why have you run away?"

"Have you been sent to take us back?" said Jonno, alarmed and preparing for instant flight as was Bomber.

Ben held out his hand. "Relax. Of course I haven't been sent to capture you or take you anywhere. I saw your school name purely by chance and couldn't resist talking to you."

"O.K, but how did you know we'd run away?" said Jonno, still somewhat suspicious.

"What else would you be doing? The boys never leave the Home without Uncles and, in school holidays you do organised activities together. Anyway, I'm guessing you have a plan, a secret destination."

"Yes, you're right, but before we tell you anymore, will you tell us some things?" replied Jonno.

"Of course I will and I bet I know some of the things you want to know. For instance, were we like you?"

"Yes, did you all have something special you were very, very good at?"

"Of course we did and like you, we passed most of our exams early, then went to the next Home for 'A' levels and preparation to go to top universities. After that, of course, we went to work in places where we could have the greatest influence."

"Do the Uncles still tell you what to do?" asked Bomber

"No, not directly, but they are still in the background, ready to help or give advice if we call them."

"How do you call them?" again from Bomber.

"By telepathy, like you do, mostly, occasionally by normal texting," replied Ben.

"Do you ever see them?" said Jonno, "I mean, in the flesh?"

"Never."

"There is one thing that Bomber and I really want to know."

"And what's that?" asked Ben.

"Why do they do all what they do, like looking after us, educating us right through uni? It must cost an absolute bomb, so they must want a return for all that money they've spent on us."

"You mean, a return for their investment?"

"Exactly, we reckon they have a secret agenda."

"You're probably correct, in fact, I'd say you're definitely correct. I think I've worked out part of the answer, but not the whole picture, by a long way," said Ben thoughtfully.

"What do you reckon they're up to?" said Jonno.

"Think about it. They make sure our gifts are really helped. They send us on the best courses at the best unis so that we are top notch at whatever we do best. We get top jobs where we are powerful and, in some cases, change things, important things. Therefore, through us, they too have become powerful."

"So what you're saying, Ben, is that they rule the country – in a hidden sort of way," said Jonno.

"I do think so, yes, in some areas," agreed Ben.

"What work do you do?" asked Bomber.

"I have a long name for what I do," he answered, "but what I am, in words everyone can understand, is a tree doctor. When I was at your Home I was very keen on Botany and while I was there I found a way of protecting the vegetables in the kitchen garden from being attacked by slugs, snails, leather jackets, greenfly and all things like them."

"But there are already pesticides like slug pellets, surely," objected

Jonno.

"Of course, I know that, but everyone, or nearly everyone, knows, too, that they are very dangerous. They are often poisonous and kill everything, the good, useful insects, too. They kill bees for a start, so that means flowers, like apple blossom, don't get pollinated and the crop fails. It's very serious."

"So what did you do?"

"I researched what people did way back, in the Iron Age for instance, and I found out they planted certain wild plants, which we call weeds, next to the crops they wanted to eat and it kept the slugs and everything away without killing them."

"Then what happened?"

"Well, the Uncles sent the report I wrote to a famous science laboratory and they tested my theory and it worked. They offered me a job there as soon as I'd finished 'A' levels and uni so that's where I am now. What I'm working on now is a way of curing trees that have caught a deadly fungus. Actually not just one fungus but lots of different fungi."

"I've heard of Dutch Elm disease and Ash Die back, but most trees look pretty fit and healthy to me," replied Bomber.

"Unfortunately, that's not the case, so I'm working on a remedy. I'm experimenting with a solution that can be sprayed as a fine mist over a wide area that will kill the fungi without harming anything else, like people, animals, insects or plants."

"Bit of a tall order, isn't it?" speculated Jonno.

"I'm getting there. Won't be long now, I hope," said Ben.

"So how will the Uncles benefit from your work?" asked Jonno.

"Good question. They have always supported me in my work and they are certainly very interested in the outcome. They are confident I will succeed and want me to get the position of Head Warden of all protected woodland and forests in Britain. This incorporates all Forestry commission land as well as the Woodland Trust. The Uncles demand that all these places are left undisturbed, so for some reason, nothing must be changed, no woods lost to housing or roads. In fact they want more woods."

"Are they just trying to be environmentally friendly?" asked Bomber.

"Possibly, but somehow, I have a feeling that they have more than that in mind, but I don't know what, not yet, anyway. By the way, what are you two extra specially good at? I'd like to know."

"Well, according to the Uncles I'm good at persuading people to agree with what I say. They say I have power over words," said Jonno.

"Then I would guess they will groom you for a position of power, possibly in the field of politics where you would certainly be able to carry out their plans.

"In a way I feel we're all being used. It's a bit creepy. It's as if none of us is able to do what we want. We're sort of -," he hesitated.

"Like puppets," agreed Bomber.

"Yes, but does it matter if you believe in what you're doing? Like me for instance, I wouldn't want to do anything else." Ben sounded as if he really wanted the boys to understand. "I have to go now," he added, glancing at his watch, "I'm off to speak at a very important meeting where I've got to persuade a committee to allocate a lot of money to my work. All part of saving trees, so wish me luck. You'd better come along, too, Jonno. You can use your word skills to make them agree," he added jokingly.

After Ben had left, Jonno and Bomber had a brilliant idea. A bus ride away, he had told them, was a country park, part of which had been converted into a 'Go Ape' area and one of his responsibilities was to regularly check the health and safety of the trees involved. The boys made straight for the bus stop and were soon on their way for an afternoon session of adventure high up in the tops of the trees. A Cornish version of 'Go Ape' was under construction not too far from the Home and the Uncles had promised a visit. They had heard of swaying rope walkways sixty feet up on the tops of trees, rope 'walls' where you had to take a leap of faith to reach them, dizzying narrow platforms, which moved in the wind, but, best of all, the zip wires which you held on to as you plummeted from the very top back to earth.

The boys were there. This 'Go Ape' promised to be as breath-taking as Ben had described it. Once fitted with harnesses, and only half listening to instructions they began climbing. The tree tops were busy, with excited shouts and screams echoing through the fairly dense foliage. Jonno was in front as they came to a scary rope walk from one tree to another. Bomber followed clutching the waist high guide lines, trying not to look down. He realised, too late, that he was not nearly as confident as Jonno, who was clearly enjoying himself. Gradually, Bomber became aware that a boy of about his own age was very close behind him, in fact he could feel his hot breath on his neck. He muttered something as Bomber hesitated at the end of the rope walk, looking down at the rope 'wall' he had to leap on to.

"Get a move on, dickhead," he said unpleasantly, "or do you want me to push you?" His voice was sneering. Bomber tried to stand aside for him to pass but instead the boy thumped him hard in the back and he yelled in panic as he flew through the air, landing awkwardly on the 'wall', swaying violently to and fro. Jonno had witnessed the whole thing and was worried. He could see Bomber's lack of confidence, so held back to help him finish the course, hoping he could make him see the fun of the whole thing and remind him there was always the harness to keep them safe, anyway. The nasty boy behind Bomber, though, looked set to spoil the whole adventure. Then, Jonno realised, a similarly unpleasant character was in front of him. The boy, about the same age as Bomber's tormentor, was obviously working with him to harass Jonno. The two had 'sandwiched' him and Bomber between them. They were enjoying the trouble they caused. Bomber was sweating with fear, Jonno was angry with both of them. The boy in front was deliberately moving slowly and then, as Jonno moved on to a flimsy platform ready to step on to a rope bridge, the nasty boy in front, pushed it so hard it swung violently to one side, leaving Jonno swinging from side to side and dangling helplessly in mid-air. Bomber was terror stricken, for himself as he visualised the same fate happening to him, and for his friend, seeing no way out.

Jonno, though, stayed calm, managed to clutch the rope ladder and hauled himself back on to it. He knew, with certainty, the two boys were out to harm them or, at least, to frighten them. He knew the harness would ultimately prevent any major harm from occurring, but he feared for Bomber who was already beside himself with terror. The boy in front had noted the fury in Jonno's eyes, his obvious lack of fear and had subsequently gone on ahead, rightly fearing reprisals from Jonno. He had, indeed, wanted to catch up with nasty front boy, to harass and frighten him but, of course, could not leave Bomber, unprotected. He, by now, was completely wrecked with terror. Nasty boy number two, chortling with evil glee, had Bomber at his mercy. Ready to push him or make rope walks swing madly, he was enjoying himself hugely. Despairing, Jonno realised there was little he could do to help, except speak soothingly and try to persuade him to move faster to escape the clutches of the following boy.

Deliverance came unexpectedly. A father and son, father in front, arrived on the scene. Father was tall, muscular and summed up the situation in a second.

"Stop messing about, you idiot," he commanded. "You're scaring that boy and if you don't shut it, I'll report you when we get down." Nasty boy, like all bullies, was quickly intimidated by a superior authority. The father pushed him aside, his son followed. He gently talked Bomber round the rest of the course with Jonno assisting in front. Bomber even managed to (almost) enjoy the last part, especially the final exhilarating wild slide down the zip wire.

On the bus ride back to the town, Bombe said, "You know, for the first time I was in a bad situation and I couldn't do anything about it. No Uncles, no time to fix my mind on finding help. I was really pooing myself up there."

Jonno was thoughtful. "So perhaps we are lucky to have the Uncles on our side. Everything that's happened so far has been sort of followed by the Uncles or something, except 'Go Ape' as you say. Could be they didn't help us, on purpose."

"You mean, so we realise how we need them?" asked Bomber. "I guess it could be."

Back in the town and unsure of their next move they went to a nearby McDonalds, simply for somewhere safe to sit and consider their options. It was busy, a good place not to be noticed. They drank a can of coke slowly, ate a burger and stayed till closing time. They decided to go to the station the next day to find out about trains to Chichester. Meanwhile, with money being scarce they found a likely bus shelter, with strong glass sides and wooden roof, fairly comfortable bench set back. They pulled on their thick sweaters and prepared for a long night. However, there was unexpected entertainment. Soon after they sat down, a young boy of about eight walked in and sat with them.

"I'm Matt," he announced. "I live over there and I told my mum I was going next door to see my friend. He's out so I've come to talk to you." He said this in a tone that suggested he was doing them a great favour. Before they could reply, he continued, "I'm on the school's student committee. I'm deputy but I do most of the stuff because the head of the committee is a girl and she's useless. At meetings she always proposes soppy things, like girls should be allowed to wear nail varnish in school. I always propose really good stuff, like we should all be allowed to have seconds at lunchtime and go in the library at break time." He paused for breath.

Jonno broke in quickly. "Did they pass your suggestions?" he asked.

"No, they didn't." His voice expressed indignation. "The headmistress said we'd all get fat if we ate seconds, which means she must eat a load of seconds," he added with a hint of venom this time.

"I'm surprised they vetoed the library proposal," said Bomber. "You'd think they'd encourage reading."

"Oh no, we don't get to read," said Matt, "We sometimes play chess or scrabble or just talk. We think the staff are being unreasonable. Just because we're young they deny our rights. I'm considering getting up a petition and I shall send it to the court of Human Rights in Strasbourg." He continued in like vein for several minutes without taking a breath – or so it seemed to Jonno and Bomber who simultaneously thought he would be an ideal student at the Home. He suddenly glanced at his watch, jumped up, saying, "I must go or Mum will wonder where I am. It's been great talking with you. I hope you've enjoyed our conversation." He ran quickly over the road, leaving Jonno and Bomber amused.

Their next visitors were the police. They were cruising slowly round the square in their squad car and pulled up at the shelter. Jonno said hurriedly to Bomber, "Usual story. O.K. We're on a walking holiday, just got enough money for the train tomorrow. Agreed?"

They didn't have to say anything, as it turned out. Two policemen left the car and came towards them. Suddenly the police car's electronic voice gave an urgent sounding message, the men turned, got back in the car and drove off with the siren screaming, the blue light flashing. "Saved!" said Jonno. "I wonder if they'll come back."

Their next visitor, however, was a young man in torn jeans, scruffy parka, accompanied by a large dog of uncertain parentage with brown soulful eyes. The man frowned as he sat near them. "This is my shelter," he announced. "The last bus went ages ago, so get out. The dog's called Snapper," he added with menace.

Bomber and Jonno were unperturbed. Their former life on the London streets had hardened them to people like this and much worse.

"Would you like a sandwich?" asked Jonno, who had a few elderly

cheese ones left in his rucksack. The young man took two eagerly
and devoured them with speed, although he gave Snapper most
of the second one. Bomber could see immediately that neither he
or Snapper were any threat to him or Jonno. They were soon in
earnest discussion about the relative merits of civil disobedience
and peaceful protest, a subject close to all three of them. The young
man told them his name was Digger, that he'd been living rough
for a couple of months, didn't like it much and would probably go
back home when the nights turned colder. His mother, apparently,
desperately wanted him to return.
"What did you do before you left home?" said Jonno.
"I'd just left uni. I managed to scrape a 2.1 in Psychology so I should
be able to find something fairly quickly in the autumn."
"Why did you do this, you know, live rough?" asked Bomber, who
couldn't imagine anyone who had a good home would deliberately
choose to be homeless.
"I thought it would be a laugh, a bit of an adventure, you know,
the open road and all that stuff. Freedom, I guess," he finished
unconvincingly.
"And was it?" said Bomber
"Not really. I like being free during the day, going where I want,
meeting people, but it's bloody cold at night, even with my padded
sleeping bag. I'll be glad to go home."
The boys told him their story – harsh life, living in squats etc. on the
streets, the dangers, hunger, perennial cold and of their rescue by
the Uncles, their education, their individual gifts.
"I can understand why you wanted a bit of freedom, a bit of a laugh,
but don't you want to go back? Sounds a real cushy number to me.
Tell me, what special gifts have you two got?"
He appeared fascinated by what they hold him about their own
particular strengths and those of some of their friends, like Tom-
Tom and Fungus. He then said something that, as the meaning of
his words sank into their minds, electrified them. From Digger's

point of view if was merely a casual remark; to Jonno and Bomber, it opened up new and infinite possibilities. A very casual remark, "Sounds to me as if you two are very rare specimens. You must be able to use that part of the brain that almost no one else can."

"Meaning?" asked Jonno.

"It's like this. We have to study the brain and its function. Didn't you know that there's a lot of the brain we don't know about. I mean we don't use it because we can't, we don't know what it does."

Of course, thought Bomber and Jonno at the same time. That explains a lot about us, Tom-Tom and everyone at the Home and especially the Uncles, yes especially them.

Excitement. A need to talk about this concept. It was thunder and lightning. A storm of ideas, powerfully there.

"Sorry Digger, we have to push on. Good to talk to you. Hope you go back home soon and keep warm. Nice to meet Snapper," said Jonno and patted the large and friendly dog who, in no way, mirrored his name.

The two moved on, reached the High Street, found an alleyway wide enough for vans to deliver goods to the shops, followed it and found they were directly behind a large department store. Jonno, turning a handle found it turned and opened on to a back entrance. Of course, they went in and were soon sitting comfortably on a settee which was part of a window display. Forgetting for a moment their excitement at their astonishing discovery – or possible discovery, from Digger's words, Jonno said, "I've always wanted to do this, sit in a window display and pretend to be one of those model things."

"Me too. This is great. We can sit absolutely still, then wink if shoppers look in at the display. I can't wait to see the look on their faces," replied Bomber, giggling.

"What Digger said made sense about us, especially about you and Letty and people like you who can do so much, like you can send messages to people and they can do things immediately, like the

Uncles arrived at the quarry seconds after you thought about them
– and there's the way you can go into the past, the present and even
the future. That must be part of the brain that no one properly
understands." This from Jonno.

"I thought that too. Digger's theory also explains why all of us at the
Home are so good at languages," agreed Bomber. "I remember we
learnt in Biology that learning foreign languages came from a certain
part of the brain which is not highly developed. Scientists think
there's a mass of things we'll be able to do in the future when our
brains get unlocked, so to speak."

"Yes, and don't you see," interrupted Jonno, eagerly, "The Uncles
already know about this. Probably they can do even more stuff than
we can."

"Such as?"

"I don't know – anything," replied Jonno, "not just mental things,
like being able to do Maths without a calculator, work out incredibly
complicated mathematical problems in their head in seconds like
Uncle John, but physical things too, like Ginger back at the Home.
Uncle Jim says he will easily win loads of gold medals in the next
Olympics when he'll be old enough to enter."

"D'you know, I reckon we can learn to time travel," said Bomber,
thoughtfully.

"You mean like in Star Trek, those old films? 'Beam me up, Scotty',"
said Jonno, laughing.

"No, seriously, I almost can, already. Several times I've thought I was
having visions, like when we first escaped I saw something huge and
it was dark all around me."

"I remember, now," said Jonno, "You went all fuzzy for a moment,
then you came back. I thought you were messing about."

"No, I wasn't and it's happened since, I'm somewhere different, then
I come back and everything's the same as before. I think Letty can
time travel too. In fact, I think we are getting stronger all the time at
moving back and forwards."

"Only some of you. I can sort of see what's going to happen more by guesswork than real psychic powers. You really are psychic."

"No, you've got it wrong. I think a few of us are able to use something deep in our brain which gives us the power to connect with time and space," explained Bomber hesitantly. "Psychic is the wrong word."

"Does your body go, too?" asked Jonno.

"I think it will," answered Bomber, "I feel as if I'm in a tunnel and, so far, I haven't reached the end, but each time the light at the end seems brighter and nearer."

Jonno suddenly felt drained. "I'm going to crash out," he said, curling up on a deep cushioned armchair. Bomber, also exhausted, did the same. Unlike Jonno he could not find oblivion. Instead his thoughts ran about in his mind in a disorderly way. He was uneasy. Dawn, pinkish in the Eastern sky, shadowy in the shop window. Bomber, alert, saw a few early workers passing by, a few dog walkers. None looked in at the boys in the middle of the display. He nudged Jonno who woke up and giggled again as Bomber had the night before. "This is a great gag. I wish the others could see us." Bomber caught Jonno's mood and they posed like models, freezing into statues when anyone came in sight. Soon the street was busier, commuters hurrying to the station, school boys and girls in neat uniform deep in conversation. Still no one noticed them. Bomber and Jonno were mildly disappointed.

"I want to see their faces when they finally do realise we're here," said Bomber. Jonno suddenly sat taut. "Look," he hissed between his teeth, "Look over there by the bus stop."

Bomber looked. He felt cold. The man and the woman with a hatchet face were looking at them. The boys jumped up, ran to the back of the shop, down another alleyway and out into a side road.

Chapter 9. Loss

"Station's this way," said Jonno.

They arrived at the station, bought tickets to Chichester and joined the throng of men, women and school pupils waiting for trains.

They didn't doubt for a minute that their pursuers would know they were waiting for a train and Jonno realised with a sinking feeling in his stomach that somehow they would know their destination was Chichester. Their train was announced. It was already almost full and as it pulled away, they were forced to stand pressed against several other travellers.

"At least they won't be able to move about very easily," said Jonno.

"Somehow, I don't think anything will stop them finding us," replied Bomber. "When we get to Chichester, I'll do my disappearing thing."

"How?" asked Jonno.

"I think myself invisible," he replied, "I become part of the scenery. Say, we're in a wood, I think of myself as a tree. I know it works, I've done it before."

"What about me? I can try but I don't think I'll succeed," said Jonno, worried.

"Don't worry, I think I can do it for you as well. Just stay right by me, as close as you can."

The train pulled into Chichester. Although its final destination was Portsmouth, at least half of the passengers left the train with the boys. The exit barrier was narrow and a great crowd pressed forward, carrying Jonno and Bomber with them. The man and woman were waiting at the barrier.

"What do I do?" asked Jonno.

"Nothing unusual. Just keep going and leave it all to me," he replied.

They were close to the barrier. Jonno had a strange sensation, almost as if he were someone else, and then Bomber said, "Come on, hurry up. We're through but I can't keep this up for long."

Jonno found himself walking into what was obviously a bus station. It was busy. Bomber said, "Do these buses go to your village?"

"Yes, I remember now. Number sixty, goes from Midhurst to Bognor and vice versa."

"O.K," said Bomber, "Which direction are we going? Hurry, before they find us again."

"Over there, look that one, it's a number sixty and it's going to Bognor. That's the one we need. It goes past the top of Runcton Lane."

They climbed aboard, the bus moved out of the bus station. It was fairly full but the man and Hatchet Face were not on board. Jonno relaxed, happily pointing out familiar landmarks to Bomber, who, in fact, was a little drained after his successful effort at 'cloaking' both himself and Jonno. He was happy, though, thinking it was a very useful skill to have and would probably serve him well in the future.

"That was brilliant," said Jonno, "You really got us past them. They must have been only a few feet away."

A few minutes later. "Come on, Bomber. There's the Walnut Tree and there's the Lane. We've finally got here. At times, I never thought we would."

Bomber could feel Jonno's excitement as they almost ran down the road, with Jonno's running commentary. "That's the ice-cream house. The person who lived there used to sell ice cream out of her front room window. It was so good, better than any I've ever tasted. And, look, here's the mill pond and there's the mill," pointing to a rather big and gloomy house over an inviting shallow mill race with jewel clear water, sliding over smooth stones with ferny fronds of water weed. Bomber could see tiny flashes of silver fish and could also see it was a place of clear enchantment. Further on they passed thatched cottages and oak beamed houses set back behind hedges, the whole village looking unbelievably idyllic like the villages in the T.V series the Uncles liked watching. Bomber wondered if there were as many murders here as in Midsomer, where everyone appeared to have a guilty secret.

"Here we are," said Jonno. Bomber saw a pretty looking house with a large bay window on either side of the front door. There was a high leafy hedge with lots of honeysuckle entwined in it almost hiding the pretty, slightly overgrown front garden. There were two more bay windows set in the roof. Bomber liked the look of it, especially the two brick pillars, each surmounted by a large concrete ball on either side of the drive to the left of the house.

"Come on, come and see Uncle Tom," called Jonno, impatiently, as Bomber stood looking at the house. He suddenly felt a faint tinge of unease, as if something was, not exactly wrong, but not what Jonno was expecting. Jonno, meanwhile, had run up the drive and knocked at the side door. A man appeared. He smiled at both of them.

"Come on in Jonno and you, Bomber. We've been waiting for you. I bet you've not had breakfast yet. How about eggs, bacon, beans, tea and toast? How does that sound?" said the man, drawing them both in and closing the door. An intoxicating smell of food filled the kitchen. A table in the middle was full of plates piled high with bacon, eggs, sausages, beans, racks of toast and a huge teapot. But the boys hardly noticed all this. Who they saw immediately on entering was Uncle Jim, sitting at the table with a plate of toast and butter. He looked completely at ease and smiled at Jonno's open mouthed astonishment.

"I can see you're both surprised," said Uncle Jim.

"That's an understatement if ever there was one. I didn't know you knew Uncle Tom," stuttered Jonno.

"Oh yes, Uncle Tom has always worked with us. In fact, it's through him that I first came to know of you and, because he was homeless with you, I knew of Bomber. You were both just the sort of boy we needed."

"Don't forget you stayed with us on holiday when you were very young," said Uncle Tom.

"Of course I haven't forgotten. It was brilliant here, climbing apple trees, looking for eggs in the long grass under the trees. Is the orchard still here and the chickens?"

"Alas, no. Time passes, things change. But you are still as welcome as you were then."

"What is this work you both do?" asked Bomber, not sure he would like the answer.

"You've already worked it out for yourselves," remarked Uncle Jim.

"We reckon it's all about our brains, that for some reason a few people can use areas which are lost to most people, even very clever people," said Jonno.

"That is correct but there is something else you must learn to accept even though you might find it frightening or, at least, disturbing," answered Uncle Jim.

"What do you mean?" said Bomber, even more uneasy.

"Something, somewhere, can lock into your minds, the minds of those like you, and use you," said Uncle Tom grimly.

"How do you mean, 'use us'?" asked Jonno.

"We are not absolutely sure yet, but we're working on it. That's why you are especially important to us, Bomber, because you, out of all our boys, are most advanced in your ability to 'cloak' yourself – very useful in espionage work and you can successfully step outside terrestrial time."

"You mean I can time travel?" Bomber said.

"That is not an accurate description," reflected Uncle Jim. "What you actually do is move outside time here, on earth, which we have invented for convenience. You move smoothly into what people call the past and the future. All time is always NOW, what ordinary people call the present. Do you understand?" he concluded.

"I think so," mused Bomber. "What you say explains lots of stuff I've been wondering about."

Jonno interrupted, "How do those two people, the man and horrible looking woman fit into all this? Are they anything to do with your organisation of Uncles?"

"Certainly not," answered Uncle Tom. "As you rightly suspected, they are members of the W.D, a rather nasty branch of the government whose main work is to do with warfare, high velocity weapons designed to kill many people quickly and, what you accidentally witnessed, mind control."

"So that's what they were doing in the quarry, torturing people?" said Jonno.

"They would call it, experimenting," replied Uncle Tom. "They certainly don't kill people. Most of the people you saw are volunteers who are paid quite a lot of money to have types of electric shock and readings taken from their brains."

"So that's why we saw people wired up?" said Jonno, shuddering. "It still looked pretty horrible to me. I wonder what they would have done to us, if they'd caught us."

"Probably simply given you a mind altering drug to make you forget all you saw down in the quarry."

"Don't worry. Bomber and Letty between them would have got you out of the mess," said Uncle Tom, reassuringly.

"So Letty and the other girls are all part of this?" said Bomber.

"Of course. You should know that. Letty is as ready as you are to intervene in human action in order to avert some disasters. She is part of our sister school," said Uncle Jim.

"What about Maisie? Is she part of all this?" asked Jonno, remembering her friendship and her assertion that he and she would meet again.

"Of course, as were all the others at the mysterious country manor. Surely you felt the glamour of it all?" said Uncle Tom.

"What's going to happen to us now?" asked Jonno.

"Well, Jonathan, or Jonno, as you prefer to be named, you will return today, with me, to the Home. All your fiends will be very pleased to see you and you can tell them all your adventures, Tom-Tom especially," replied Uncle Jim.

"Bomber as well," said Jonno.

"No, not Bomber, not yet. He is going on a journey beyond time to try to avert a terrible event."

"What event?" said Bomber, and, at the same time, felt excited at the strangeness and wonder of everything.

"We don't know that, only that it is of vital importance to us all that you go. You will understand your part – and Letty's, when you arrive."

"Letty is coming with me?" said Bomber, feeling relieved and pleased. "When do we leave?"

"Now, before it is too late."

Jonno said, "I will see him again, won't I?"

Uncle Jim replied, "I'm sure you will. One day."

Bomber was gone.

Jonno's cheek was wet.